THOUGHTS
FROM A GARDEN SEAT

VOLUME 3

Thoughts

From a Garden Seat

VOLUME 3

by
Derek Turton

Published by Derek Turton
158, Sancroft Road,
Spondon,
Derby,
DE21 7LD

British Library Cataloguing-in-Publication data
A catalogue record for this book is available from the British Library

ISBN 978-1-8381893-2-7

Printed and bound by Jellyfish Solutions Ltd

*This book is dedicated to the memory of Jean,
to all my family, and to my sisters Pam and Ann*

*Special thanks to Revd. Peter Dawson OBE
and Shirley, whose words of wisdom have kept me
on the right pathway.*

*Also to all who have been affected in any way
by the COVID Virus.*

Teach me your ways, O Lord;
Make them known to me.
Teach me to live according to your truth
For you are my God, who saved me.
I always trust in you

Psalm 25 v 4–5

Contents

About this Book

In March 2020 the UK along with the rest of the world, was launched into the turmoil of the COVID pandemic. The effects of the Pandemic impacted in one way or another on everyone resulting in a time of stress and concern across communities.

In an attempt to cushion that impact, the author of this book wrote a series of reflections, some spiritual, some factual, some humorous, which were published in a book, *Thoughts from a Garden Seat*, Volume 1, as a compilation of these reflections. The book was an outstanding success with all available copies sold.

Following the success of Volume 1, a second book, Volume 2 was produced which equalled the previous publications popularity.

This book, Volume 3, is a continuation of the reflections over the third six months of the COVID crisis. The thoughts and memories stimulated by the reflections have proved to be a lifeline to many who have been isolated or housebound as a result of the national restrictions. It has also proved to be a gateway to Bible Study and understanding of some of the scriptures.

This book will continue to stir the memories of the past, challenge our priorities of the present, guide a pathway to the future through the scriptures and give hope and assurance through our Lord Jesus Christ.

About the Author

Derek Turton was born in 1948 and is a born and bred Yorkshireman, originating from the northern town of Bradford and his experiences of life in the 1960s will strike a chord with many readers of that era. After leaving school at 15 he worked as an apprentice bricklayer in his father's building business but left to enter Local Government in 1969, a career that would last over 40 years. Derek migrated south to Derby in 1973 and still lives in a suburb of the City.

His experiences as a Fellow of the Royal Institute of Chartered Surveyors, a Justice of the Peace (both now retired) and an active accredited Local Preacher have provided him with an insight into many sides of life some of which are reflected in this book.

Derek's wife Jean, died in 2012, and he has been well supported by his three daughters, seven grandchildren and great granddaughter.

After his family, Derek has a passion for vintage farm tractors and classic cars and can often be seen driving one of them along the country lanes of Derbyshire or at many of the rallies held in the area.

This is his third book in a trilogy, the first two books being Volume 1, which proved to be extremely popular, and Volume 2 which surpassed the first book in its popularity.

Volume 3 is a product of the demand from readers and has been eagerly anticipated.

Foreword

Revd. Peter Dawson OBE

In the third volume of his reflections from his garden seat, Derek has written a book that is unputdownable. His skill as a writer reaches new heights. His sense of humour in relating tales of everyday life cheer the spirit.

Accounts of how things used to be remind readers of going to what used to be called picture palaces, of waiting for the rag and bone man, of using a kettle that whistled and of being warned by mum after misbehaving to just wait 'till your father gets home. The author's parent's response as the growing lad came home with winkle pickers on his feet echoes events in many households. At every point, readers of a certain age are led into a world they once knew.

Equally arresting but right up to date, is the authors description of the arrival of one hundred cricket. His clever use of this to analyse the significance of numbers in scripture is well done. There is a hilarious account of the arrival of the sat nav, and its unintended part in a funeral service.

The author's clever use of his tales to reveal messages in the Bible means Bible study groups will love this book; so will anyone wanting to reflect on life in its many ironies and on the deeper meaning of ordinary events. This book, as the saying goes, gives you something to think about.

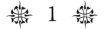

1

Great Expectations

Micah 5 v 1–5   Isaiah 53 v 4–9
Isaiah 61 v 1–2

I have to admit that I was never a fan of Charles Dickens novels when I was a youngster. I think they were a bit too dark and depressing, although I do recall we touched on Oliver Twist in senior school English Literature lessons, but I preferred the musical version.

However, recently I watched a television programme on BBC 4 where a presenter dissected a classic novel and analysed what the author was actually saying. One of the books featured was Charles Dickens's *Great Expectations*.

I was fascinated to learn that within the files of one of our universities, they have the original hand written manuscript of Dickens's notes of the book. Apparently, the book started its life as a love story but in the words of the programme presenter, 'Love stories were not Dickens's forte', so it was changed it into a sort of mystery story. Consequently, large sections of the original text had been crossed out and re-written. One such section was the opening chapter.

The original opening of the book placed the main character, Pip, in an orphanage having lost his parents. The published version placed Pip in a graveyard at night (what did I say about being dark and depressing?), where he is accosted by a terrifying escaped convict called Abel Magwitch, who demands that Pip goes off and steals him some food.

The story then develops as Pip becomes the recipient of a mysterious legacy and takes the opportunity to learn how to be a gentleman. The love story bit returns when Pip strikes up a relationship with a strange character called Miss Havisham, and her adopted daughter, Estella, a cold, very proud but beautiful young lady of Pip's age. At this stage all the evidence misleadingly points to Miss Havisham being Pip's mystery benefactor.

Through twists and turns, including the murder of Pip's sister, we eventually discover the true identity of the benefactor of Pip's finances and move towards the end of the story, which suffered many crossings out and re-writing in the original manuscript.

In true Dickensian style, his first ending was depressing and involved the death of several characters, including Miss Havisham being killed in a fire. Estella was married twice and was not happy, while Pip remained single, and was not happy. However, in the final version, although the death count remained the same, Pip and Estella are brought back together and there is a vague suggestion that they may be successfully joined at some time in the future.

Another interesting fact is that when the import was first published, it was in the form of a serial, almost like EastEnders or Coronation Street, each instalment published in a newspaper owned by Dickens. Each episode left the reader in cliff-hanging suspense as to what happened next. This was to encourage readers to buy the next episode and the ploy was undoubtedly successful as sales of the newspaper reached an unprecedented high and saved it from bankruptcy.

The analysis of the book asked the question, 'Who was the subject of the Great Expectation?' Was it Pip, Estella, the benefactor or Pip and Estella together? I will leave you in cliff-hanging suspense.

There is no doubt of the expectation on the shoulders of our Lord Jesus Christ. His path through his ministry and to the cross had been written centuries before his birth. The manuscript suffered no alterations or re-writing and the ending was always predicted and in accordance with God's will.

The prophet Micah predicted the birth of Jesus in Bethlehem and his genealogy to King David. The prediction gave great expectation, not only to the people of Israel, but to all people on the earth who will see the greatness of God and will experience peace through the Messiah Jesus Christ.

Isaiah 61, places the great expectation of salvation firmly on the shoulders of Jesus. These words from the Old Testament were used by Jesus himself to describe his ministry, to bring good news to the poor, heal the broken hearted, release captives, give the prisoners freedom, and release all believers from the power of sin.

There would be opportunities for Jesus to re-write his destiny, to take away the cup of poison and to avoid that ultimate journey to the cross, but he followed his Father's will and fulfilled the prophecy to give up his life so that we can have life.

I feel strangely warmed in the knowledge that Charles Dickens crossed out his thoughts and re-wrote his manuscripts. I have re-written this reflection three times.

2

Stick to me Like Glue

Romans 8 v 38–39

In 2020 my son in law and his brother and sister, decided to launch a new venture by taking over an empty shop unit in our village and opening a DIY store. The shop unit had previously been a Building Society so many of the fixtures and fittings could be retained and as COVID restrictions at the time permitted, I went to help with the erection of racking, shelving and display stands which then needed filling with the products that were for sale.

When the shop opened I spent some time guiding customers around the sales area and advising on various products. A lifetime in the construction industry began to pay off and I haven't enjoyed myself so much in years, but unfortunately COVID restrictions eventually put a stop to my involvement.

One thing that did impress me about the shop was the vast range of products that are available for those people who wish to do home improvements for themselves. Take adhesives for an example. There are a multitude of adhesive products suited for every conceivable situation. Wallpaper adhesives for light weight papers, heavy weight papers, water proof papers, and even an adhesive that is coloured pink so that you can ensure that everywhere that needs to be pasted has been pasted.

I can remember a song about when father papered the parlour, you couldn't see him for paste.

There are adhesives that will stick anything to anything including fingers to fingers if the necessary safety precautions are not complied with.

But it can get confusing. I had a customer who came into the shop asking for glue that would stick glass. I showed them a couple of suitable products, and then I remembered a range of adhesives with a trade name of Gorilla. I am sure that one of these would be suitable, I assured them, and Gorilla is a very good product.

The look of disgust on their face was unmistakable and the reply was that rainforests were being destroyed by that stuff. As the logic behind the statement escaped me I moved on to the Evo Stick.

All of today's modern adhesives are very efficient and convenient, some in tubes with dispensers and most ready to use. Many years ago I can remember my dad boiling up a solid block of glue in a pan in our cellar at home when he was making window frames. The smell of the boiling glue was revolting.

I can also remember a TV advertisement for well-known wallpaper adhesive where a pair of overalls was pasted to a board, a man climbed into them, and he was lifted up by a helicopter to demonstrate the strength of the product. I always admired the man's faith in the product, or was it all a trick?

In Paul's letter to the believers in Rome he reassures them of the power of faith in our Lord Jesus Christ which will adhere them to God. Romans Chapter 8 verses 38 to 39 is the culmination of Paul's explanation of how faith in Jesus ensures that nothing can separate us from the love of God.

Paul is anxious that the believers may feel insecure about God's love when they replace the Law of Moses with their belief in Jesus Christ so he searches and lists everything in life that could be seen to alienate us from God. His list includes, trouble, hardship, persecution, hunger, poverty, danger and death.

He concludes that only sin could isolate us from God's love but sin had been overcome by the sacrifice of Jesus Christ on the cross. God sent his only son to be the sacrifice that will give us salvation.

The outcome of Paul's search is to prove without doubt that nothing can separate us from the love of God. No other message can give us more security and hope for the future than that.

Noel and Tricia Richards wrote these words in their song of praise,

Now by God's grace we have embraced
A life set free from sin

We shall deny all that destroys
Our union with him
Nothing shall separate us from the love of God.

Years ago while at college I visited a factory that produced a specific type of glue from animal bones. The process involved boiling the bones of animals to extract a basic ingredient of the glue. The smell was unbelievable and even worse than my dad in the cellar at home.

I wonder if the customer in the shop thought that they boiled up Gorilla bones to make Gorilla glue.

I'm sure they don't.

3

It's not God's Fault

Job 1 v 13–22

Bill Brown gazed wistfully at his new car parked on his new drive. It was all that he had secretly wished for but never dreamed that he would own. It was a bright red Mercedes that glinted in the sunshine. The paintwork resplendent and highly polished while the chrome glistened and reflected like mirrors. The sleek lines of the sculptured body swept Bill's eyes from the front to the rear of the car absorbing every angle and curve. It was a million miles away from the Ford Fiesta that he had previously owned for the past twenty years.

He lifted his gaze to take in his new house that provided the perfect backdrop that framed the car as if in a portrait. The house was a four bedroomed detached property over-looking Headingly Cricket Ground. Bill and his wife Marjorie had purchased it a year ago but had only just moved in. It was so different to the three bedroomed semi-detached that they had left in Armley on the outskirts of Leeds, but, everything in life was now so different to those days living there.

Five years had passed since Bill opened his redundancy letter from United Insurance and he had filled that time by dedicating himself to writing his books. To his surprise he had become a very successful author and no longer could he be considered as average. So why, as he gazed upon the fruits of his success, did he feel anything but happy. Why, deep down, did he wish to return to being, Bill Brown (Post Dept.), United Insurance.

So many events had overtaken him in those fleeting five years. His son, Bill, had left to attend university in Edinburgh where he had passed out with a commendable degree in Chemical Engineering but rather than return home, he decided to stay on for further studies and after successfully obtaining employment with an oil company chose to remain north of the border.

Bill's daughter Susan left home for Bristol University and is now studying for a BA in Liberal Arts. While at Bristol she met and fell in love with a young man and now shares a rented flat with him.

Bill had contemplated many times how quiet the house had become without the children, and he found himself missing their youthful banter and even their teenage problems.

Two years ago Bill's wife Marjorie was called to urgently visit her elderly mother who had suffered a major fall. Unfortunately, due to her age, the fall resulted in serious injuries from which Marjorie's mother could not recover and she sadly passed away in the hospital. Since then Marjorie had been withdrawn and suffering from depression. Despite great effort Bill had found it difficult to communicate with Marjorie and did not know how to deal with the situation.

Bill had discovered success in writing, success in a new career, success in financial security but he constantly yearned for the happier times when he was Mr. Average.

The Book of Job is the story of a good man who suffers total disaster. He was rich in every sense of the word, materially, spiritually and through his family. Most of all he was a righteous man who tried to fulfil all his responsibilities to God in his way of life and in accordance with God's will.

Just when Job was congratulating himself on being so successful and obviously in God's favour, disaster struck.

In just one day Job lost all his oxen and donkeys in a terrorist attack that also claimed the lives of his servants. In another attack he lost all his camels and also those servants but even worse was to come as in a freak wind storm all his family were killed and Job was on his own.

Despite all these disasters Job never lost his faith in God even when his friends tried to mislead him with poor advice, although, Job found it difficult to comprehend why the disasters were happening to him when he had been such a righteous man. He questioned God and begged for an answer but even in his questioning he never blamed God for his demise and accepted that bad times will fall upon all people at some time, and it is not God's fault.

Eventually God blessed the last part of Job's life in recognition of Job's faithfulness and he lived to a very great age and had another large family. Also his wealth was reinstated even greater than before.

Bill Brown sat at his desk, opened an A4 ledger, picked up his pen and began to write.

'It's not God's Fault'
An autobiography, by Bill Brown

✻ 4 ✻

Take up Your Arms

Judges 7 v 1–8

I have just completed reading Captain Sir Tom Moore's autobiography which is a fascinating read. Although there are obvious differences, there are many parallels between his life experiences and those of my own father. I suppose it is inevitable in many ways due to their similar age and therefore generation.

Both were Yorkshire men, Capt. Tom being born in Keighley and my dad being born in Barnsley but moving to Bradford, a stone throw from Keighley. Both had suffered bereavements at an early age, my dad lost his mother and sister while Capt. Tom lost his uncle.

I have to admit I know very little about my dad's childhood, I don't think he shared a great deal even in conversation when we worked together. I know his father (my Big Grandad), remarried after the death of his first wife, and had quite a large family to his second wife creating a second generation of siblings to my dad and his immediate brothers and sisters.

As was the case with most men and boys in the Barnsley area at that time it was expected that as soon as age permitted they finished up underground in the coal mines (down t'pit), or at best working on the surface but still at the colliery and dad was no exception.

Then comes another parallel with Capt. Tom, motorbikes.

Dad used to tell the stories of his adventures on his Matchless 1000cc bike as a youth with similar experiences to Capt. Tom on his motorbike. I think dad still had his bike when he met my mum but I don't recall either of them indicating that mum ever rode on it. It is interesting that despite dad's passion for motorbikes, he strictly forbade me from having one. To this day although I have driven most types of four wheeled vehicles, I have never ridden on a motorbike.

Similar to Capt. Tom, dad's passion for motorbikes was pivotal in his role in World War Two. Dad used to tell the tale that after conscription and basic training; officers asked if any of the new recruits could drive. Dad put up his hand but failed to disclose that he had only ever driven a motorcycle. He along with one or two other men, were taken to one side and presented with the keys to an extremely large tank transporter, which was a very big articulated lorry specifically designed to carry tanks. For the majority of the war, dad, and his tank transporter, where in North Africa transporting new tanks to the front line and bringing damaged tanks back for repair.

Captain Tom, first had command of a tank then moved to be an instructor in tank warfare, but he was stationed in Burma.

There was a time when dad was re-introduced to a motorcycle but details of this escapade were always sketchy both from dad when he was alive and research after his death. It involved dad acting as a dispatch rider on a motorcycle but whatever the purpose behind the operation or the eventual result of the action was never revealed. It earned dad a mention in dispatches and he was honoured with an Oak Leaf to add to his medals.

I noted that Capt. Tom also had a similar experience as a dispatch rider for which he was also decorated for his actions.

On de-mob dad chose not to return to his previous employment and attended a rehabilitation course in building construction at Thorpe Arch near Harrogate, something that was to be the blueprint for his employment for the rest of his life.

Dad and his three brothers started a building business called, 'Turton Brothers' and carried out building work across the Yorkshire area. In the early 1950s dad decided to go it alone and formed his own business which he ran until retirement. Capt. Tom on the other hand returned to his father's building business.

If we read the Bible, Judges 7 verses 1–8, we see that there were even stranger methods of selecting suitable soldiers for battles. Judges describes the period in Israel's history after the death of Moses and Joshua, but prior to the introduction of their monarchy. Over this period several notable people established themselves as great leaders and 'heroes' (Judges) of the Jewish nation. One such leader (Judge), was Gideon.

Gideon had the unenviable task of facing the mighty army of the Midianites and he started to recruit his own army to attack the enemy camp. He successfully achieved assembling a force of 22,000 soldiers before God intervened, instructing him that if he followed God's instructions there would be no need for an army of that size. When the army would have victory they would claim it for themselves and not accept that it was down to God's power that they succeeded. God wanted an army of just 300 men to destroy the Midianites, and then it would be clear to everyone that God is powerful.

The selection process involved taking out all those who were afraid, those who did not want to be there, and those who drank water from the river in a certain way (lapped the water up with their tongues). Eventually God had selected 300 men from the original 22,000 for Gideon's army.

Gideon followed God's instructions and armed his men with a trumpet and a glass jar containing a torch and by creating fear and confusion they drove the Midianites into a frenzy and they began to fight amongst themselves.

Notwithstanding the fact that dad rode a motorcycle, drove a tank transporter, drove army surplus trucks and vans for the business and a car for himself, he never passed a driving test – and you could tell.

His driving licence came from the army and entitled him to drive just about everything.

❈ 5 ❈

Ireland ⌒ From Darkness to Light

Nehemiah 2 v 1–5

There are many aspects of Ireland that fascinate me. I love Irish music, the intoxicating blend of Irish pipes, fiddle and drums. The Irish language, as with the Welsh tongue, is lyrical and from the throat so different to the English. I find the Celtic influence intriguing particularly in their art and religion but also I find the past turbulent history of the Irish people both interesting and disturbing. From battles with invaders, to famine and persecution, to mass exodus to other lands and the internal turmoil of recent years, throughout history I think the people of Ireland can best be described as bruised but never broken.

Despite my interest in Ireland, I have never visited the South but I have journeyed to the North of Ireland on three separate occasions.

My first visit was in the mid-1970s at a time when the involvement of British troops as peace keepers was at its height. Along with one or two other youth leaders I accompanied a group of teenagers, who had successfully won their way to the finals of a national quiz organised by the Methodist Association of Youth Clubs (MAYC), to the previous year's quiz winners in Northern Ireland.

The finals were held in a place called Dungannon, not too far from Belfast. We flew from Luton airport to Belfast, and then boarded a coach for the short journey through the city to a boarding school in Dungannon which would serve as our accommodation and the quiz venue.

Driving through Belfast it was hard not to notice the boarded up shops, bars and restaurants that had been the victims of the bombers and similarly in Dungannon we passed the burnt out shell of what had been the main post office. Evidence of the army presence was unavoidable with fortified towers and barbed wire in the streets of some parts of the town. One evening we came across an army patrol moving through the town centre. The soldiers looked to be not much older than the teenagers we had brought to the quiz.

The atmosphere in the town felt very uncomfortable although there was nothing that could have been interpreted as being threatening, in fact the enthusiasm and hospitality of the Irish organisers was second to none.

My second and third visits were both to the City of Belfast, the first to a National Conference and the second to a 'Core Cities' meeting representing Nottingham City Council. These visits were in the early 2000s and the difference that thirty odd years had made was remarkable. The centre of the City had been transformed since my Dungannon experience, with new shopping complexes, leisure facilities, hotels and a state of the art conference centre which doubled as music venue. During our visits there was no sign of any military presence, or was it that we were we not taken to the relevant areas of the City?

Nehemiah was a troubled soul. He was living at a time when the Jewish nation had been scattered across Babylonia, with only a few 'undesirables' left in the ruins of Jerusalem. Nehemiah had been fortunate insofar as he was serving the King in his palace as a wine waiter (slave), but his thoughts constantly took him back to the city of his ancestors.

When news reached him from Jerusalem to say that despite the passage of many years no work had been done to restore or rebuild the ruins, he was devastated. He knew that God was calling him to return and rebuild the City walls but would the king permit him to leave the palace and go? Not only did the king give his permission for Nehemiah to go, but he also gave him letters of authorisation in order to obtain materials to complete the work.

We could say that Nehemiah is the patron saint of project managers as he successfully returned to Jerusalem and in the power of God he organised teams of people to rebuild the City walls, despite facing opposition from rebels.

When the work was complete the scattered nation could return to the place of their ancestors and their spiritual home where God could reside with them again.

After the quiz in Dungannon, which incidentally we lost, we returned to Belfast via a visit to a peat bog, where we viewed some artefacts that had been uncovered. We then boarded the plane to return to Luton. On arrival we were met by anxious parents as it transpired that after we had left Dungannon for the Peat Bog there was an incident in the town that was reported on UK television news.

We were oblivious to the event but parents were very aware of it.

6

Staff Shortages

John 10 v 11–18

Let me introduce you to my staff.

Now you may, at this point, be expecting to me to introduce you to my typist, my researcher, my typesetter and my distribution team, but as I don't have any of these people at my disposal, I would only be introducing you to myself.

So, let me introduce you to my staff.

I purchased it in 2018, from a National Trust shop at Hunter's Inn in Devon. I was on holiday with my daughter, my son in law and my two grandsons and staying at a farm near Paracombe. Leading from the farm was a footpath that eventually led to Hunter's Inn and then on to Hells Mouth, a secluded bay and rocky outcrop jutting into the sea.

We had undertaken several walks during the week and all had terminated in a steep incline to reach the final destination. Now I really enjoy walking – downhill – but I'm not over keen in walking uphill especially, as so often happens, that by some act of mischief it appears that someone increases the incline of the path making it far steeper coming back than it was on the outward journey (or so it feels).

I had noticed that some of the more experienced and hardened walkers had enlisted the help of walking sticks, modern light-weight aluminium with plastic accessories and nylon straps to wrap around the wrists. These sticks obviously propelled the walkers up the steepest slopes as they all seemed to pass me with minimal effort. In view of this revelation I decided that it was time that I invested in this simple but apparently effective aid to my fell walking and where better to buy one than from a National Trust shop one of which happened to be at Hunter's Inn.

Unfortunately, on searching the shop I discovered that the world and its wife had also decided to purchase the before mentioned sticks leaving only an empty rack where the sticks should have been displayed. However, not accepting defeat I rummaged around at the farthest corner of the shop and found the one and only walker's staff. It was made of Ash (the label said so), and was 1.6m (5 feet) long with a metal shoe at the bottom and a hole drilled through the top to house a leather strap to go round the wrist. This was far more superior than a 1m (3 feet) long aluminium stick with plastic appenditures, this one was the real thing and it was for me.

When I had recovered from learning the price, I paid the National Trust volunteer the money (she gave me a complimentary bag as I had spent so much), and left the shop better prepared to face the rigours of the return journey and that soul destroying final incline.

It is surprising how walking with a staff adds to your confidence and agility and as we continued our walk towards Hells Mouth I began to depend more and more on my new purchase. The rhythm of the tap, tap of the metal tip to the staff on the stony rocks gave an assurance that we were making progress. It also became a source of annoyance to the rest of the walking group and earned me the nickname of, 'Long John Silver', or 'Gandalf' from Lord of the Rings.

It was when we ascended the steep incline leading back to the farm that the staff came into its own. Periodically I could stop and lean on the staff for support while I had a well-earned breather.

Jesus said, 'I am the good shepherd', not any shepherd but the good shepherd. In saying this he emphasised that he would do anything to protect his flock. He would never desert them when danger threatened; he would never leave them hungry but would lead them to the greenest pasture. He would never see them lost or not knowing which way to go and would lay down his life for each one of his sheep.

The Shepherd always has his staff or crook and Christian art often depicts Jesus as the good shepherd with his staff ready to guide and protect, support and lead us through life and its storms. The hired shepherds work only for money and don't own or care for the flock. When danger comes they will run away and leave the flock to the mercy of the wolves, but Jesus never abandons his sheep, he knows each one as his father (God) knows him and he knows the father.

In the autumn of 2018 I returned to Paracombe, along with my trusty staff, by myself and spent a few days walking the footpaths. While walking a narrow road I came across a herd of sheep (well two or three) that had escaped from their field. By stretching out my arms and my staff, doing my best Adam Henson on BBC Countryfile impersonation, I helped the farmer retrieve the escapees.

I'm relieved it was not his bull that had escaped.

7

Friends

John 20 v 19–23   Galatians 2 v 1–10

As the mist rises above the road map of the government's plan for easing the COVID restrictions during the coming year, we have the opportunity to reflect on the effect of the pandemic on our lives.

Without doubt our lives have changed and I am sure that some of the changes may stay with us. Working from home, for example, is now a permanent feature of working procedures for many people and internet trading is now almost the norm. Groceries home delivery, once a common service (Granville in Open all Hours), then became extinct, but now is much sought after again.

One aspect of life that has been subjected to great pressure is that of friendships. Eighteen months of social separation has resulted in many friendships being put on hold, with people not meeting, not sharing, and not maintaining that social link that is so important.

My daughter is a keen fan of the television series, 'Friends' (now only available on specialist channels),

The story line revolves around the escapades of a group of young friends, totally different in characters, as they battle with the ups and downs of life, often leading to hilarious situations. The important message in the series is that they all support each other no matter what happens. The strapline being, 'I'll be there for you'.

The importance of friendships is something that is often overlooked but it is clinically proved that we need good friendship connections to maintain our mental and social wellbeing. Friends can celebrate good times, and support during bad times. Friends can help to prevent loneliness and give an opportunity for companionship. Friends can increase a sense of belonging and purpose.

I have to say that all my friends from my school days are no longer in touch and as I moved around the country I have lost track to where they are now. In my teenage years I spent most of my time with a friend Ian Norris. We were totally miss matched, he was tall and I was short, he was very intelligent and I was not, he came from a wealthy background and I did not, and he was two years older than me, but we had some great times. Unfortunately I lost touch with Ian in 1969 and despite several efforts I have never been able to trace him.

As with many people Jean and I had special friends who after over fifty years I still keep in touch with on a weekly basis, even through the COVD crisis.

Our families have grown in parallel and we have both experienced great celebration and sadly disasters, but as the saying goes, 'A celebration shared is doubled and a disaster shared is halved' (I have no idea who actually said or wrote said that). I can't wait for the time that I can arrive at their doorstep with an overnight bag and shatter the peace and tranquillity of their home.

Possibly the strangest group of people to become friends were the disciples. Most of them came from different backgrounds with different skills and experiences of life but during the three years of Jesus's ministry they learnt from his teaching, developed spiritually from his preaching and were influenced by his love for each one of them. In return they devoted themselves to Jesus and with the exception of Judas, returned their love for him.

The disciple's friendship developed into interdependency, so much so that after the crucifixion we find them gathered together in a locked room supporting each other, hiding from the authorities, trying to make sense of what had happened and of what to do next. It would have been easy to scatter across the country, individually blending into society anonymously, leaving the past behind and staying safe. But they chose to support each other and carry on the work as Jesus would have wished.

It is interesting to note that that in Paul's letter to the Galatians, Paul relates to a meeting in Jerusalem with the disciples Peter, James and John. This meeting is likely to have been twenty years or so after the death of Jesus indicating that the disciples were still a friendship group at that time.

As Ian Norris was two years older than me, he passed his driving test before I was even old enough to drive. He bought a 1936 Morris 8 car in which we travelled all over the country for various reasons. Unfortunately the car regularly broke down and as we had no AA recovery, Ian's dad was frequently called out to come and rescue us from some remote place. Eventually Ian's dad threw in the towel and gave him his mum's car a nearly new Mini which was much more reliable – not as much fun though.

8

Mixed Messages

Galatians 4

Due to the slight relaxation of the COVID restrictions that have recently been introduced, I had a visit from my daughter and my great granddaughter, Imogen. She is eighteen months old now and I have not seen her this year, apart from images on a mobile phone screen. We had a really enjoyable afternoon in my garden, thankfully in warm sunshine.

They arrived about noon and departed about two thirty during which time Imogen never stopped running circuits of my garden, pushing a push-along car around the lawn or being pushed on a three wheeled trike around the lawn. Even in periods of, 'rest' she insisted on diving in and out of a pop up tent pretending it was a swimming pool. I have no idea where her energy came from but it was certainly not on a low tariff.

Eventually, it was time for them to leave and go home and as my daughter fastened the straps of Imogen's car seat, there was a suggestion that Imogen would probably be asleep before the car reached the end of the road. I have my doubts about that, but it is quite possible that I will be asleep before the car got to the end of the road.

After they had left I reclined in my garden seat with a cup of coffee and realised why God, in his infinite wisdom, has designed human beings to have children while at a relatively young age. It is obviously the only time of life that they can keep up with the antics of their offspring.

However, this does not obviate grandparents from more sedentary responsibilities in the upbringing of their grandchildren and at some point in time the inevitable question will arise, 'Grandad, what do you know about long multiplication and division?'. Of course the answer has to be, 'I know everything about long multiplication and division,' after all I am Grandad. At this point the homework books suddenly appear accompanied by paper and pencils and grandad begins to regret such an impulsive reply to the original question.

Not to be deterred, the pencil glides across the paper and zeros are moved to the right and decimal points are moved accordingly and low and behold an answer appears at the bottom of the page, followed by a look of bewilderment and a statement of, 'We don't do it like that at our school.'

Then follows a lesson on how they calculate such mathematical problems, 'At our school,' with vertical columns appearing and disappearing along with numbers and zeros, and eventually, as if by magic, the answer appears at the bottom of one of the columns.

'That's the answer.' The child eagerly points with the pencil, and with a slightly smug smile adds, 'And its right.'

I am speechless. It's the same answer that I arrived at.

How could the education authorities have the audacity to change the method of calculating long multiplication and division after sixty five years without consulting me?

It has to be said that the home tuition, that has been recently imposed on many parents, does have its dangerous side, as mixed messages and variations in methods of working, can inevitably be confusing for the young student. It is for that reason I always stick to, 'How it is done at our school'.

Mixed messages are something that is a recurring problem for Paul in his letters to his churches, particularly in his letter to the Galatians. Paul's theology that he preached to the predominantly gentile congregation in Galatia was built around justification by faith in Jesus Christ, the good news of the gospel. This theological message was welcomed by the believers but in Paul's absence, false teachers with Jewish allegiance, preached that believers must obey the Law of Moses before they could be one with God. As this was diametrically opposed to Paul's teaching there was obviously confusion in the minds of the believers.

Paul maintained that the Law only served to highlight the sins of the Jewish nation and that through the death and resurrection of Jesus Christ, our sins have been forgiven. Accordingly it is through faith in Jesus that we are saved and are one with God.

It was a complex issue, difficult to understand for the Jews so even more difficult for the gentiles. Thankfully as Christianity spread globally, Paul's theology was accepted as being in line with that of Jesus Christ and the claims relating to the Jewish Law were overturned.

My grandchildren are now all grown up and past the need for assistance in long multiplication and division. Conversations have now changed and terms such as 'The Law of Probability' and 'Quantum Physics', and 'Calculus' roll readily off the tongue (theirs not mine). Even the gestation cycle of a dairy cow is an acceptable subject over Sunday tea.

But Grandparents have a secret weapon called, 'Wisdom'. It is wise to listen, eat your meal and at the earliest opportunity, change the subject.

9

Coronation

Matthew 26 v 6–13 *2 Kings 9 v 1–3*

I was saddened by the news of the recent death of Prince Philip, the Duke of Edinburgh. I had never actually met him but liked him, more admired him rather than liked him. I always felt that he married Queen Elizabeth for the right reasons and not for the glory that accompanies being part of the monarchy. When that time actually came, it was necessary for him to give up his own career and his naval ambitions to become an escort to the Queen of England, a role that did not even have a job description at the time, but he carried out his duties for almost seventy years.

Obviously, as part of the television tributes to his life, there were many references to the Queen's Coronation in 1953, and the accounts of that occasion brought back many memories for me and my sisters. I was only five years old at the time but strangely I have some recollections of the event and my sisters filled in some of the gaps.

We were living in our mid-terrace house in Lidget Green, a suburb of Bradford, and I can recall my mum talking, over the garden wall, to the next door neighbour about the death of the King and the excitement of the imminent coronation of the new queen. The celebrations were very much a communal event but I seem to remember that my dad, along with our neighbours, were heavily involved with the organisation of the street or even the neighbourhood, party and entertainment.

Before any celebrations could commence we watched the coronation pageant on the wonder of television. We didn't have a television set until much later, but a neighbour further down the street had one so we all piled into their house to watch history being made. It was a very small black and white television set in a wooden cabinet with sliding doors that could be pulled across when not in use. The picture quality was not brilliant and the sound was at best scratchy, but we thought it was magical.

As great as the television experience was, for us as young children, the main event was the neighbourhood party in the Methodist Chapel Hall in the centre of the village (next door to the Second West pub).

The hall had been decked out with flags and bunting, and trestle tables had been set up around the room, laden with food, sandwiches, cakes and jelly etc. Bench seats had been provided to accommodate more people, or perhaps we didn't have any chairs, it didn't seem to matter. At one end of the hall there was a stage and much of the entertainment came from there. Communal singing was in abundance. My dad always fancied himself as a singer and never missed an opportunity, much to the embarrassment of the rest of the family. I vividly recall dad picking me up and standing me on the stage to sing a popular song of the day. It may come as a surprise to learn that not a word passed my lips as I defiantly stood there in silence, much to the annoyance of my dad, until someone else's son or daughter came to my rescue and sang the song.

I can remember that we all had special red, white and blue paper hats with The Queen's picture emblazoned on them and of course we all had union jack flags to wave. We also received a cup with the Queens picture on the side, and some people received a propelling pencil with red, white and blue stripes and a crown on the top.

In the Old Testament the sign that a king had been chosen by God was when a Priest or a Prophet anointed the king with oil. This ritual was the pouring of holy oil over the head of the chosen person and as the oil flowed from the head down onto the rest of the body, so the Holy Spirit flowed also. Initially the act of anointing was restricted to any object or person who worked in the Temple such as cups, vessels and Priests but when the Hebrew people decided on the need for a king, the anointing was extended to include the chosen King reflecting the holiness of God's chosen person.

Jesus is a King, not only a King but a King sent by God. He was already Holy because he was God's own son, but the woman (thought possibly to be Mary Magdalen), in Matthew's Gospel wanted to recognise Jesus as a King by anointing him with the expensive perfumed oil. This oil was usually reserved for preparing a body for burial, but the woman was anxious to use it symbolically while Jesus was still with them. She wished to show that, to her, Jesus was her King, Lord and Master. This act of love took place shortly before Jesus was arrested and led to death on the cross. The anointing was brightness against a dark and threatening backdrop.

I am almost sure I have, in the loft, a Coronation Cup with a picture of the Queen on the side. I'm not sure if it is actually mine or someone else's that I picked up on the day, after all I was only five years old, one cup looks very much like any other when you are five years old.

✤ 10 ✤

Bread on a Bank Holiday

1 Kings v 8–24   Galatians 5 v 7–11

There is nothing worse than a wet Bank Holiday Monday. Outdoor activities are limited and those plans for a family outing are shattered. As a youngster, my mum always had a range of suggestions for me to adopt on such occasions, get out your colouring books and pencils, get out a nice book to read, tidy your bedroom, or even worse, sort out your toy box. None of these suggestions were appealing or capable of breaking down the physiological barrier of disappointment and boredom.

So it was on Monday 3rd May 2021 when the rain poured down, the wind blew a gale and the temperature dropped, that I decided to take a leaf from mum's book, not to do the bedroom or the toy box, but to attack the kitchen cupboards. Tidy them all up, put new wallpaper offcuts on the shelves, something past down from my mum and my mother in law, and throw away any unwanted items.

I started with the food cupboard. It is surprising what you can find at the back of a food cupboard.

An opened jar of pickled onions dated 2018, which was opened on Christmas Day and then forgotten, a packet of bread sauce mix of the same era, and a Tupperware container, containing the remnants of a packet of Cornflour from an unknown date and time. Then there are the small glass bottles of herbs and spices, Bay leaves, now dried, withered and crispy, Cloves, probably from Christmas 2018 partnered with the onions, and some unknown brown powder without a label.

Having successfully negotiated the food cupboard, I then turned my attention to the other side of the kitchen and the cupboards that are less frequently visited. These are where the electrical goods which were on special offer at the time of purchase, reside. These include, the, 'Juicer', which is a gadget for extracting juice from fruit etc. to make a refreshing healthy drink, we bought it at the start of our healthy eating initiative, used it once to see if worked, then put it in its place in the cupboard. It lives alongside the handheld food mixer which is a twin to another food mixer in the adjacent cupboard. Also in there is the toasted sandwich maker and a box of accessories for the hand held food mixer that never seemed to fit properly. Beneath all these snuggly sit the two coffee making machines, one more elaborate than the other, but used just as often.

However, the crowning glory must go to the bread making machine, which I hasten to add, has been used on several occasions. It is a remarkable piece of engineering which with little effort produces quality results. Simply load into the non-stick box the required amounts of flour, milk, salt, butter and yeast, switch on and in an hour and a half, as if by magic, you have a loaf of bread. The house is filled with the aroma of baking bread which triggers a yearning for hot freshly cooked bread and butter.

There are several references in the Bible to bread making and yeast but one that attracts me is the story of Elijah and the widow in Zarapeth. The action takes place at a time when the entire region was in the grip of a severe drought and famine. Food was scarce and ingredients for the very basic essentials such as bread were simply not available. Add to this scenario a poor widow and her son with just enough flour and oil to make one small loaf of bread, hardly sufficient for the son, after which they would face death by starvation, and we realise the impossible situation in which this woman found herself. Despite this, as she recognised Elijah as being a holy man, she agreed to share what she had with him.

As with everyone who sacrifices themselves for God's work, the widow was rewarded with a seemingly endless supply of flour and oil, enough for her needs and her son and Elijah for the duration of the draught. The widow would also witness God's love when her son took ill and died, but was raised back to life by God through Elijah.

Both Jesus and Paul used illustrations of yeast in relation to the spread of evil in society from a small start to infect many people.

Paul's letter to the Galatians points out that a small amount of yeast can make a dough rise to twice its size. In the same way evil will from a small source spread amongst society, but the love of God is more powerful and will overcome the source of all evil.

The problem with my bread maker is that the fresh baked bread is so tempting and inviting that you just can't resist the temptation to try some while it is hot, which results in trip to the local Coop store to buy another loaf for tea.

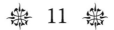

11

Give us a Hug

Galatians 2 v 6–10

I think it would be true to say that if the COVID restrictions had existed when I was a youngster, I would have probably breathed a sigh of relief. Not just because school would have been cancelled, but also because it would have put a temporary hold on Sunday visits to relatives. Most Sunday afternoons were taken up by loading all the family into dad's truck or van, whichever he had at the time, and setting off to Rothwell near Leeds or Wakefield, to see mum's relatives.

Now, due to dad's role in the war he left the army with a driving licence but never actually passed a driving test and this was evident in his style of driving. Add this to the fact that mum had a very nervous disposition, the Sunday excursion inevitably degenerated into a nightmare journey of mum trying to persuade dad to slow down, not to drive so close to other cars, and to try to avoid every pot hole in the road.

I was permitted to take a toy with me, the intension being that on arrival at our destination, it would keep me quiet. This was successful for a short time but even the most favourite toy becomes tiresome after about twenty minutes, then it turns into a nuisance factor. If the weather was fine dad would take me for a walk round the garden but it was a very small garden. Eventually it came to the time go home, but it was also the time for hugs and kisses. I would hear mum shouting, 'Come on Derek, give Grandad and Aunty a big hug and a kiss until next week', and my heart sank into my boots. The aroma of moth balls, the overenthusiastic grip on the shoulders, the wet kiss on my ear, because I had turned my head away, were all a repeat of last week. I have never been one for hugs and kisses and I blame those experiences of family visits in the 1950s. However, in my more mature years I do recognise the value of such physical contact and recent news of the lifting of the restrictions on giving and receiving hugs from family and friends, is welcomed. Although the relaxation may appear to be insignificant in the great scheme of the return to normality, it is actually a major step forward.

Medical evidence has proved that giving and receiving a hug or an embrace has a positive effect on our mental well-being, lowers blood pressure, and increases our sense of security and assurance that we are not alone.

Of course it is not just hugs that have been prevented, handshakes have also been banned. They have been replaced with touching shoulders or elbows which, as well meant as they may be, are no substitute for a good firm handshake. Symbolically a handshake has very serious computations none less than, we shake hands with our right hand, which historically is our sword hand. Consequently, you can't attack someone with your sword if you are shaking hands, unless you happen to be left handed or ambidextrous. In some business circles the hand shake is still recognised as being an indication of an agreement. As we sign a contract, then an agreement is also binding through a handshake but it can also be a gesture of welcome, friendship, farewell and an offering of peace.

Despite regaining the freedom to embrace our family and friends, we are still reminded of the caveats that need to be applied. The danger from the spread of the virus has not left us and care is still needed. Avoid facial contact, embrace outdoors, restrict hugs to family where possible, and take extra care with people who are particularly vulnerable to COVID. (Source: Government Website).

In Paul's letter to the Galatians, he relates to a meeting that took place between him, Barnabas, and several of the disciples. The meeting revolved around Paul's right to describe himself as an apostle, and his theology used in preaching to the gentiles. Paul had been open to criticism that he was not one of the twelve so could not be an apostle. In addition his theology of salvation by faith was in contrast to that of the Jewish converts and of Peter, James and John.

Throughout the meeting Paul maintained that he had met with the risen Lord Jesus face to face (Damascus Road), and it was Jesus that commissioned him to preach to the gentiles. Accordingly he had every right to use the title of Apostle. Similarly his theology was no different to that preached by James and Peter to the Jews.

The meeting agreed that Paul is an apostle, accepted his theology and agreed that he should preach the gospel to the gentiles. The agreement was sealed with a hand shake, and no doubt an embrace.

Well I am going outside now wearing my face mask to give my grandchildren a big hug. The only problem is they are so tall I need a box to stand on.

12

Contrasts

Luke 14 v 1–6   Galatians 3 v 15–18

I enjoy watching a television programme on BBC 4 called, 'The Joy of Painting', where an artist called Bob Ross, creates a landscape masterpiece with apparently little effort. During his presentation he uses a number of short sayings for advice to his students. One such saying is, 'Put dark on light and put light on dark', making the point that contrasts are important in order to make the whole picture stand out.

This made me think of how often contrasts interject into our everyday life in order to make our life's picture stand out. There is no corner of our life that is not affected or influenced by this phenomenon, our choice of food, fashion, music and opinions – now there is a cauldron for discussion, the contrasts of opinions.

Over the centuries there have been wars generated from a contrast of opinions. My dad had a saying, 'The whole world is queer bar thee and me – and I'm not sure about thee'. What he meant to say is that his opinion was right and the rest were all wrong. I hasten to say that this was not always the case, after all my opinion was the right one and he didn't always agree with me.

There are some areas where contrasts are more prevalent than others, for example, in between young and old generations, fashions, religion and politics. I think that when God granted us the ability to have an opinion, he didn't take into account the political arena.

As in the Law of Physics there is an equal and opposite force, then in politics there is always an equal and opposite contrasting opinion. This seems to regularly descend the Houses of Parliament into chaos between the governing party and the opposition. However, this freedom of speech and clash of opinion is central and essential to our democratic system of government and from the apparent chaos raises the right decision – although that depends on which side you support.

I must say that I recently came across a news item that left me confused and concerned about human nature. It was a news report by an Indian dentist practicing in India, who had contracted the COVID virus. She was young and not from the poorer sector of the Indian community. In addition she worked in the clinical environment of the hospital but she had still contracted the virus. In her video clip she was pleading with the countries of the world, including the UK, not to be complacent when it appeared we were successfully beating the pandemic. The virus was still there and had to be recognised and her desperate situation was evidence to this.

The following news item involved a man standing outside a theatre. He was bitterly complaining about the government restrictions that prevented his choir from performing at the theatre behind him. He obviously considered that as the number of infections had reduced considerably, the government should relax the restrictions that prevented the theatre from opening.

Two contrasting opinions both moulded by the situations in which the participants were involved.

I should point out that the young dentist in India passed away shortly after making the video appeal.

The Bible is a book full of contrasts, good against evil, reformation against tradition, life against death, and opinions. In Luke's Gospel we find Jesus invited for a meal at the home of a leading Pharisee. The Jewish leaders already knew about Jesus and had no doubt witnessed some of his miracles and acts of healing. The invitation was unlikely to have been made as a friendly gesture as we are told that everyone was watching Jesus closely. It becomes even more suspicious when a man with swollen arms and legs happens to approach Jesus but Jesus sees through the Pharisee's plot and turns the tables asking the Pharisee what they would permit under the Law.

The act of healing is not the issue here, but when the healing took place, that is on the Sabbath. Jesus points out that if oxen (a valuable animal) needed to be rescued on the Sabbath that would be accepted. The man was even more valuable than the oxen so is it not right that he should be saved?

Paul in his letter to the Galatians had a similar problem with the Jewish leaders. Paul preached that to be one with God (Justification), depended on faith in Jesus Christ. Through faith we can live our lives in accordance with the gospel and share in the Good News of Salvation.

The Jewish leaders violently disagreed with Paul saying that Justification can only come from compliance with the Law of Moses. Paul takes them back to Abraham who was in favour with God before the Law was introduced therefore was Justified by faith and not by acts of works.

I recall, as a young teenager, coming home after purchasing a pair of black suede 'Winkle Picker' (long pointed toe) boots with a Cuban heel. I thought they were the best pair of boots on the planet and I had shown then to my friend and enjoyed the look of envy on his face. Surprisingly my mum and dad did not share my enthusiasm. 'Nice' young people did not go round wearing such shoes, and they would only lead me into trouble. In addition, that style of shoe would disfigure my feet for the rest of my life.

I still wore the boots until the Cuban heels had worn down so far that walking was impossible, anyway they were so out of fashion by then.

13

Our Cup Runeth Over

John 4 v 7–14

Back in 1966 when I first met my wife Jean, her mum had tea, coffee and biscuits delivered to her door by a company called, 'Ringtons'. When Jean's mum and dad moved to Derby in the late 1970s, then so did Ringtons and they still continued to deliver tea, coffee and biscuits to their doorstep. After mum and dad both passed away I didn't have that heart to cancel the Ringtons fortnightly visits, so guess what? They still deliver to me, it is almost a tradition. Obviously the van has changed and the driver, but the nature of the service has still remained after all these years.

I don't know if they still supply loose tea any more, but as they supply speciality teas it is quite possible that they do, although I have tea bags.

I think there is something about a cup of tea that is refreshing, even on a hot day, reassuring when you need to think through a problem and also the panacea to any state of emergency. No matter what the crisis may be, the first step in rectifying the situation is to put the kettle on for a cup of tea.

As a young man I always drank my tea and coffee with both milk and sugar, however, when I left school and started work, invariably building sites were devoid of either milk (that was not 'off'), or sugar so my taste changed to having both beverages without any additives. One thing that I do find unacceptable is tea made in a cup and not in a tea pot. At home I have a very small tea pot for use when I am by myself and I always make the tea in the pot and pour it into my cup. To me it never tastes the same when the tea bag is placed in the cup and the water added, however, I don't go through the very British procedures of warming the pot first before adding the tea and the final hot water, or making sure that the water is still boiling when poured on the tea, or any of the other idiosyncrasies that go with making the perfect cup of tea.

I understand that in some Eastern cultures making a cup of tea is quite a long and elaborate process which results in a very small cup of tea. Some techniques involve letting the boiling water cool slightly to allow oxygen back into the water, or pouring the tea from a great height to achieve the same result. At the end of the day it is all down to a matter of taste and as we are all individuals our tastes differ.

For example, before noon I tend to drink tea but after noon I usually drink coffee. This differs from other members of my family who require coffee at breakfast to kick start the day. Other aspects can influence our tea drinking experience and the taste. Does filtered water make a better cup of tea than tap water? Does the shape of the cup or mug affect the taste of the tea? Why, when having multiple cups of tea, does the first cup taste better than all the others? How long can a tea pot be allowed to stand before the tea is undrinkable? Is a cup of tea brewed or mashed?

In this world of intense and complicated technical solutions to almost any question or conundrum, why can't we answer the question of how to make the perfect cup of tea?

In John's gospel we find Jesus and the disciples walking on a long and tiresome journey from Judea through Samaria, to Galilee. In that part of the world and at that time of year, it would have been cool in the early morning but quite hot by mid-day.

We are told that the disciples had ventured off to find food in the adjacent town of Sychar and Jesus had found his way to a spring that formed Jacob's well. It was noon (12.00 Jewish time and 18.00 Roman time) and the temperature would have been reaching its height. Together with an early start, a long journey and the heat of the day, Jesus would have been tired, hot and in need of refreshment.

At the well he met with a Samaritan woman who had come to draw water. Her presence is of great significance for several reasons. She was a lone woman with no companions. It was the hottest part of the day and not a time people would be usually drawing water. She met a man (Jesus) not only a man but a Jew who spoke to her and asked for water.

It is possible that this woman was a social outcast which could give an indication of why she was there in these circumstances, and she had brought with her a water pot to fill. The water she would drink would refresh her physically but not spiritually.

In this passage we see Jesus reaching out to win the soul of this woman and to set her free from the spiritual prison that she was in. He brought her to realise her needs and also offered to her the solution to her problems. He offered her forgiveness, salvation and freedom, true refreshment which would last her lifetime.

Possibly for the first time in her life she was not condemned, judged or ridiculed, but was offered love and forgiveness.

When Ringtons call the driver always has a little speech to promote the special offers on that week. These can range from special offers on biscuits, boxes of cakes and so on. On his last visit he offered me a special pack of hand cream and body lotion.

I tactfully explained that I had little use for a large bottle of body lotion but I could make good use of a packet of double chocolate chip cookies.

❈ 14 ❈

The Circle of Life

2 Corinthians 5

The song, 'The Circle of Life' was composed by Elton John with lyrics by Tim Rice, for the 1994 Disney animated film, 'The Lion King'. The film then spread to the theatre/ stage and has been a tremendous success, along with many of the songs from the film/ show.

The circle of life is very interesting, building on the philosophical concept that we all start and end in the same place. Our lives, from beginning to end resemble a complete circle. No matter how big or small the circle is, it ends in the exact same place for everyone.

Of course the song was composed for the film which had a story line about a young lion cub and its journey through innocence to being the rightful king of the jungle, with many twists and turns along the way. Accordingly, for the purposes of the film, the circle of life relates to the lion cub's birth through to his rightful inheritance and his status in society, leading onto the future through the birth of his own son.

Naturally we can apply the same philosophy to our own lives and our circle of life. When we are very young we celebrate our birthdays with a traditional birthday party, inviting friends of a similar age, to devour copious amounts of sandwiches, cake, jelly and ice cream. When we reach our late teenage years we celebrate being eighteen years old (21 in my day) with similar party celebrations, often with the same friends but with the addition of a different type of beverage. We then find ourselves receiving invitations to weddings (or civil partnerships), often followed a few years later to baptisms and christening parties.

All too soon, retirement parties creep onto the scene, these tend to be a little more sedate than the previous celebrations but none the less an important signpost in life's circle. Sadly the next stage of the circle is not considered to be as joyful as the earlier milestone celebrations. Recently I have had the need to console two people who have lost partners in the final stage of the circumference of the circle.

Just as the baptisms, the birthdays, the weddings, and all the other stages of life, the funerals appear to come round far too frequently once they start to appear and no matter how strong and convincing our beliefs may be, the loss of a loved one is inevitably a bitter pill.

My mum had her own philosophy at times like these to help her come to terms. She found consolation in the belief that for every person who passed away, a new child was born. If the person had not moved on there would have been no room for the new child and another circle to begin. It was certainly the case when she passed away as only a few months after, our first child was born.

Paul has a wonderful theology on death and life everlasting which he brings to the believers in Corinth in his second letter Chapter 5 verses 1–10.

He reflects on our earthly bodies being only a tent; don't forget he was once a tent maker. He points out that a tent is a temporary structure, fragile and vulnerable to damage. It can be repaired and patched up to keep it going for longer.

The tent was recognised as being a temporary home for the Nomads, a tribe who drifted across the wilderness, a home that could be taken down and re-erected in a different place.

But eventually the fabric would wear out and no longer be capable of being repaired. It would then be buried in the sand to decompose and return to dust from where it came, and so it is with our earthly bodies at the point of death.

God's spirit was breathed into the clay to give life so it is by God's spirit that we live.

The clay (tent), may return to dust but the Spirit is not destroyed; it comes from God so it can never be destroyed. It is not the product of any human hand, it is divine and as such it is raised from the tent and ascends into a heavenly home in God's kingdom, a home with no suffering, no decay, and no death, described by Paul as being the eternal heaven.

Paul describes that he has no fear of suffering and no fear of death because he knows that he will eventually share in that heavenly home along with his Lord and master. At that time, he will start a new life in the home that God has provided.

Perhaps it could be described as being the new circle of true life.

During the COVID lockdown I have tended to dress, 'casual', as being encouraged to stay indoors I found little incentive to get, 'dressed up'. However, as I was returning to the pulpit I thought that I had better try on my suit to make sure everything was still okay. A strange thing had taken place – my 'tent' had expanded, particularly round my waist line.

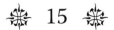

15

School Uniforms ∼ Always Label Them

Isaiah 41 v 10   Matthew 28 v 20

I was having a conversation with a group of friends recently, over a cup of coffee, and we started to discuss school uniforms. Sometimes it is difficult to establish where the source of the conversation originally derived from but on this occasion it was one of the group that admitted to still having his school cap. Not only did he still have the cap after over 60+ years but it also still had his name label stitched inside.

I have a vivid memory of my wife Jean, sitting in a chair stitching name labels inside articles of clothing that made up the school uniforms. Sweaters, skirts, blouses, ties, socks, blazers all had to be labelled, but when that had been achieved, she would turn to the PE kit with the shorts, shirts, pumps, socks and other items. The whole operation then had to be repeated three times as we had three daughters.

The favourite location for the label was, for the sweaters and blouses, at the back of the neck, and for the skirts and shorts, on the waist band, however this only generated complaints that the labels were, 'itchy' and irritating so Jean had to be more imaginative as to where she fixed them.

The problems arose after the first PE lesson when more often than not someone else's name was on the PE kit that returned home. The following day at the school gates the mums would embark on a PE kit exchange programme in an attempt to correct the situation. At the end of every half term or full term the school would place a box full of lost items of uniform for mums and dads to rummage through in the hope of recovering their offspring's school wardrobe, some items did not have a name label to help the process.

As frustrating as the school uniforms could be, it was insignificant compared to the labelling of the Brownie and Guide uniforms. This entailed sewing on badges which were required to be in specific locations and interrelationships with other badges. In addition all the badges had to accord to a diagram handed out by Brown Owl, and no one argues with Brown Owl. When the conundrum, which is second only to the Rubrik's Cube, had been mastered, only then could the matter of the activity badges be addressed. These badges were stitched individually down the length of both arms of the tunic. Enthusiastic Brownies and Guides could harvest more than enough badges to fill both arms and have some left over for the camp blanket. What joy, a camp blanket.

I must admit the school uniform problem was just the same when I attended school. Neck ties were a particular issue, I recall that at the end of the day's lessons the first thing to do was to rip off the tie and stuff it into your pocket. There always were one or two ties on the floor at the bus stop outside the school and the Caretaker's job was to collect them up and add them to the lost property box. If your name was on the tie then you got it back, if your name was not on the tie you were in trouble for not wearing a tie, in trouble for losing it and in trouble for not having your name on it in the first place. I always had a spare.

One thing I did like was the school blazer. We never had one in junior school but we did in senior school. It was dark blue with the school coat of arms on the pocket and underneath the heraldry was the school motto, 'Labor Omnia Vincit', which translated into, 'Work Conquers All'. The headmaster told us that the quotation would remain with us all our lives and as I can still remember it, I suppose he was right.

I have a set of pictures of Christian art from across the world. The countries include Africa, India, China, Japan, South America, Cameroon, North America and the UK. The art work depicts various scenes from the Bible, many of the Nativity and of the Crucifixion. It is interesting when studying the pictures to realise that the facial features and dress of the subjects reflect the appearance and culture of the people in the countries where the artist originated.

For example, the artwork from Africa depicts Jesus as being black, whereas in the artwork from China and Japan Jesus has an oriental appearance. The UK paintings depict Jesus and the surrounding countryside, to be quintessentially British.

Our God is a personal God who is with each one of us constantly and through Jesus Christ and the Holy Spirit dwells within our hearts. Accordingly it is natural for the artist's work to reflect the perception of the personal God. We see Jesus as being like us as he is within us, God made us in his image so we see him as an image of ourselves.

In both Isaiah and Matthew's gospel we find reassurance that God and Jesus are with us until the end of time no matter how bad the world about us appears to be. We are never alone because Jesus knows our name and God will protect each one of us and take us into his house for everlasting life.

School ties in my day were quite broad at the widest point but the fashion trend in the 1960s was for slim line or even bootlace ties. To interface school with fashion we reversed our tie to make the broad part tuck into shirts out of sight allowing the narrow tail end to cascade from the collar. It was a bit of a compromise but we thought it looked trendy.

16

Water Power

Exodus 14 v 21–29

Recently I have enjoyed watching a programme on BBC 4 television where the entertainer, Griff Rhys Jones, has been renovating a 200 year old farm in Wales. The working farm aspect he has left to the farming experts, but the process of renovating and converting the various buildings has been the real subject of his involvement. He has been assisted by various advisers including his son who is a trainee architect.

The buildings consisted of a farm house, cow sheds, barns and a disused water mill, all of which are seriously dilapidated and in need of extensive repair and restoration. One particular building which is to be converted into a house was so wet and damp that green moss was growing on the walls and floor, which was curious as there was no apparent reason for such a bad state. It was after the first spell of heavy rain – yes, it does rain heavily in Wales, that the reason for the damp became apparent. The small stream, that in the past served the water mill, actually ran through the middle of the proposed house, in fact the small stream manifested itself as a torrent by the time it had passed through the property.

It is not the first time that I have come across this phenomenon and it is quite common when converting old farm buildings. Friends of mine bought a farm in Yorkshire which was in a hillside location. When heavy rain fell they opened the back door of the farm house and the front door and simply let the water flow through the house, it was less disruptive.

Another common occurrence when converting farm buildings is to discover a deep well under the floor and I know of several that have been retained and made a feature by placing a reinforced glass floor over the well to enable a view down to the centre of the earth.

Often the topography of the terrain around the farm and the historical purpose of the buildings can give a clue. The Welsh farm for instance had a water mill and was located in the bottom of Welsh valley, signs that could suggest the possibility of water. Subsequent investigation also disclosed the presence of a bridge.

In Derby City Centre, the Silk Mill Museum sits on top of a long since filled in mill race (millrun or mill leat if you come from the South West), which was a series of channels that diverted water from the river under the Silk Mill to drive a water wheel.

I have also been told that Buxton Opera House also straddles a water course which in times of heavy rain runs directly through the building under the floor, and legend has it that the musicians in the orchestra pit need to wear wellington boots and stand their chairs on boxes especially when playing Handle's Water Music.

Experience has proved that the worst course of action in such cases is to attempt to stop the flow of the water with some kind of barricade. Water has a very determined nature and a power that demands respect. I have witnessed brick walls, erected in an attempt to divert a water course, totally destroyed by the force of the water fighting to retain its natural original course.

When I first came to Derby in 1973, my office overlooked the River Gardens and the River Derwent weir, a view that was often entertaining particularly after prolonged stormy weather. To observe someone's garden shed sailing gracefully past my office window was not unusual or a large tree and occasionally a dead animal.

Despite the powerful and potentially destructive nature of water, we read in the Bible of several instances when God has shown his almighty power in taming this wildest of nature's characters. The Red Sea can be the most unpredictable stretch of water, with dark depths, and sudden violent storms generated by the ever-changing direction of the wind.

It is not surprising that the Hebrew people in Exodus 14 looked upon their predicament with trepidation. Before them they faced the turbulent water of the Red Sea, and behind them they felt the hot angry breath of the king's army with their fearsome weaponry, horses and chariots. We could sympathise with the Hebrews as in fear they contemplated which death was the least painful, the murky waters of the sea or the piercing blade of the soldier's sword.

They started to have regrets in leaving their slavery but memories tend to distort the truth of the past. In their distress they underestimated the power of God, he would never desert them or give up on them after bringing them this far. God's authority reaches out even into the depths of the sea and in obedience to the word of God the waters part and allow the nation to pass from slavery and death into freedom. For the Egyptians, the price of persecuting the Hebrews and the years of disobeying God had to be paid and as the waters returned to their normal levels the army perished beneath the waves.

Griff Rhys Jones overcame the problem of the river running through the house by the introduction of underground pipes and culverts but he had another problem even more difficult and from an even more powerful source. It took him two years to obtain

Town Planning permission. Who said that the pen is mightier than the sword – or in this case mightier than the JCB.

❋ 17 ❋

Which Way Now?

Matthew 4 v 18–22   Matthew 5 v 3–12

During lockdown my car has generally been an ornament on my drive and has not moved for several weeks at a time. However, recently I had the need to start it up and drive to a destination which I had not visited for two or three years. It was obviously a job for the Sat Nav (Satellite Navigation), but as always I refer to my trusted map book to establish the basic route in my mind, then I can rely on the Sat Nav for the final intricacies of the journey.

It was while I was preparing for my little excursion, that I was reminded of a story that I came across recently.

It related to a young minister and his wife who were stationed to a particularly rural circuit. As they were both ignorant as to the roads and places in their new area, they decided to invest in a new piece of technology called a Tom Tom Sat Nav. This was a small gadget that adhered to the car windscreen by a rubber sucker and connected to the cigarette lighter on the dashboard by a dangly wire. After being programmed with the address of the proposed destination, it would verbally guide the driver of the car to that destination. It was a positive breakthrough in modern technology and much sought after by undesirables who would break into cars to steal them.

The occasion arose when the minister's wife had the need to attend a funeral at a church she had never visited before. This was a job for the new Tom Tom Sat Nav device, the minister advised his wife and he volunteered to set up the equipment. He fixed the gadget to the windscreen of the car, plugged in the dangly wire and entered the information for the destination, he even pressed the start button on her behalf. All that remained was for her to follow the verbal instructions.

'Don't forget,' the minister told his wife as she set off, 'unplug the Tom Tom and put it in your handbag when you get there, and clean the ring left from the rubber sucker off the windscreen. We don't want anyone breaking into the car.'

All went well and she arrived at the church in good time. She removed the Tom Tom and cleaned the windscreen, just as she had been told to do, and went into the church. The service was reverent and respectful and it wasn't until the mourners were invited to come to the front and place their hands on the coffin which was in front of the Altar, that things started to go awry.

As our heroine placed her hand on the coffin a voice from her handbag stated loud and clear that she had, 'Reached her destination'.

Trying to act nonchalantly she turned to walk back to her seat, at which point the voice in her handbag told her to, 'Make a U-turn when it was safe to do so.'

Deeply embarrassed she crept outside and drove home hoping that perhaps no one had noticed.

We have a Sat Nav that guides us along the paths of life, it is called the Bible. In Matthew 4 verses 18–22 we can read the blue print for a way of life with all the instructions and guidance needed for our journey. Not a journey that seeks power and authority which is so often demanded in our secular expectations, but a journey that seeks humility, generosity, caring, kindness and love. A journey that guides us not be insular and possessive, but to seek out those who need help, the poor, the disadvantaged and abused, so we can in turn guide others to the love of God and to support those who are less fortunate than ourselves.

It is a Sat Nav that will at times tell us to do a U-turn, tell us we are on the wrong path, and correct us when we deviate but if we follow the instructions we will arrive at our destination in our heavenly home in the Kingdom of God.

In Matthew 5 verses 3–12, Jesus met with the first disciples and gave then a message which was the most significant and important guidance of their entire life.

Now he reiterates that same message to each one of us and we can't underestimate the impact of that guidance in our lives.

Jesus said 'Come and follow me'.

The problem with the Sat Nav is that it often fails to keep up with changes to new road layouts or the status of some new roads. I sometimes travel from Derby to visit my sisters in Lincolnshire and as I drive along a new by pass near Lincoln my Sat Nav tells me that I am driving across a ploughed field, destroying hedges and narrowly avoiding cow sheds. However, I am reassured by the fact that I am surrounded by a multitude of other vehicles that are doing the same.

I always take the opportunity to shout at the Sat Nav and tell it that it is wrong but it never admits that it made a mistake and it never says sorry.

18

Through the Eyes of an Artist

Philippians 2 v 5–11

Living in Bradford in West Yorkshire in the 1960/1970s it was difficult to avoid the name of David Hockney. He is one of the most influential and successful artists of the 20th century and is still making his mark in the 21st century.

David Hockney was born in Bradford, just as I was, but there the similarity ends. His father was employed as a clerk in various businesses in the city but always had an interest in being an artist, even attending night classes, but never achieving his goal. However he encouraged his son to enter into the art world where he was more successful than his father. David had without doubt an amazing talent and even when he was at art school he was able to sell paintings to earn extra money. This was the start of a career that would lead him to the accolade of selling the most expensive painting ever at auction – £70 million – an achievement that has since been overtaken.

David Hockney has never been shy of controversy and openly discussed the fact that he is gay, something that in the 1960s required considerable courage, he was also a conscientious objector during World War II and worked as a hospital orderly for his time of conscription. Despite all this, allegedly the most controversial decision for many people was his move from Yorkshire in 1964, to California in the United States. However, he refrained from severing all ties with the great county and retained several properties, including a studio, in Bridlington (not much different, California and Bridlington, both have the sea).

David has been profoundly deaf since the early 1970s and has relied on hearing aids from 1979. In a television interview in 1986 he revealed that the hearing problem has made him insular and to some extent antisocial as he finds large gatherings of people difficult to deal with due to the noise being generated. However he believes that after losing his hearing he has experienced an increase in his visual perception of colour and light, almost as though the colours were speaking to him, not through sound, but through sight.

In the same interview, David was asked why his style of painting and mix of palette appeared to have changed since his early Yorkshire portraits. He explained that his art reflected how the subject spoke to him and the light and the colours in California spoke differently to those in Yorkshire. On occasions when he returned to Bridlington his work would reflect the lush greens and reds not experienced in California. He explained that the product that emerged from the canvas was a depiction of what he sees through his eyes and through his senses which may not be as other people would perceive.

When asked what influences him most in his art, David replied, 'Life', his perception of the natural world, water, landscapes and also his experiences and observations of people their behaviour, posture and emotions. All these aspects interrelate within the artist's senses and are manifested in whatever the artwork may happen to be.

In Paul's letter to the Philippian's, chapter 2, he attempts to explain to the believers how they can influence other people through their behaviour and their way of life. He urges them to live in harmony with each other and not to display aggression or unrest. They must share the same love, caring and kindness so that others will see the love of God shining through their actions.

He explains that the attitudes they display should adopt the attitudes and attributes of our Lord Jesus Christ. He holds up before the eyes of the Philippians the example of Jesus Christ as a portrait of a selfless mind, a sacrificial mind, a serving mind and a mind that consistently puts others first.

Charles D. Meigs wrote;

Others, Lord, yes others.
Let this my motto be.
Help me live for others.
That I might live for thee.

May this be the perception of us in the artist mind.

In 2018, at the age of 82, David Hockney watched the unveiling of his artwork in a window in the North Transept of Westminster Abbey, artwork that celebrates the life and reign of Queen Elizabeth II. The vibrantly coloured window depicts the blue skies and a winding pathway through the Yorkshire Wolds.

It just goes to prove that once a Yorkshireman always a Yorkshireman.

❄ 19 ❄

Peonies and Hollyhocks

Ephesians 4 v 1–16

My front garden contrasts with that of my next door neighbour. She carefully and tenderly, tends to her garden, regularly clearing any weeds, pruning and replanting as the seasons progress. I tend to have a philosophy that encourages self-preservation in my garden plants so they have to survive on their own efforts with minimal intervention from my hands. Accordingly my plants tend to be more robust hardy annuals and a little larger in size to do battle with the weeds.

One plant that we do have in common is a Peony, my neighbour has one under her front window and mine is against my front boundary wall. My neighbour's plant flowers in early May, while mine flowers in June/July so between them they provide a splash of colour over several weeks. Despite the difference in flowering time the plants follow the same pattern of development. Stage 1 is the appearance of thin delicate stems projecting upwards from the main body of the plant. These develop and become stronger as they reach upwards like long fingers. Stage 2 is the evidence of a bulb like tip on each stem, a bulb that changes shape into a dark green ball which eventually ruptures allowing the brilliant red flower head to unfold from the darkness of its ball shaped prison into the freedom of the bright sunshine.

The blooms are amazing and expand to reach 75mm–100mm (3 inch–4 inch) diameter and appear to shout at people who walk past the house because people often stop and talk to them. At its peak the display is a volcanic and violent explosion of vermilion red.

But the Peony has a self-destructing design fault which manifests itself in stage 3. The blooms become so big and heavy that the stems have difficulty in supporting the weight. Combine this with the predicable heavy summer downpours and the stems capitulate and form a tangled confusion on the edge of the lawn. The petals lose their lustre and the colours fade. In the past I have attempted to support the stems with canes but never with much success and each year is a repeat of the previous year's devastation.

I have had more success with the Hollyhocks, or Foxgloves, I'm never sure which, they have established themselves against the front porch and when in full bloom their display is also breath-taking. They too have long gangly stems that reach up 1.5m (4ft 6 inches) high and produce a mass of trumpet shaped blooms along their length with colours ranging from Peach to Cardinal red. Despite this symphony of colour, the Hollyhocks have the same design fault as the Peony, the vulnerability of the stems. However, my plants have found help and support from an unlikely source. They have grown adjacent to the rainwater downpipe from the porch roof. A short length of string from the stem to the pipe gives more than enough support to keep them in place for the duration of the season. An unlikely and unnatural pairing of resources that gives the opportunity for the natural world to benefit from an unnatural infringement into its world.

When Paul established the churches in Corinth, Ephesus, Galatia, Philippi and Rome, he faced a multitude of problems, but none greater than the opposing cultures of the assemblies that came together. Paul was introducing Jesus Christ and the theology of one God, to a mix of people who previously had worshipped either none or a multitude of various gods and beliefs.

The Greeks had their own selection of gods, the Romans had a god for every occasion, the Jews had the Law of Moses and the pagan Gentiles chose any piece of wood or piece of stone. The Church of Christ introduced a new theology and a comprehensive self-support regime between its believers. In his letters Paul stresses the importance of all believers to live in harmony, helping and supporting each other, understanding each other and working together in the spirit of God. It was truly an unnatural pairing of resources but it was essential for the future of the Christian Church. Other people who witnessed this socially supportive way of life would see the glory of God shining through the believers.

God loved his creation so much that he gave his only Son as a sacrifice so that we can live. If God showed that love for us then should we not show the same love and support for each other?

During the recent COVID crisis we have witnessed many examples of lives being changed and saved by support from unlikely sources. From physical help to spiritual support, from a hand held in a desperate moment to a listening ear in a time of distress. From a friendly voice in an apparent cruel world, to a prayer from an unknown voice into a lonely wilderness.

Some years ago I purchased a tractor that had languished in an orchard for over twenty years. A sapling had rooted itself under the derelict machine and using the metal chassis as support had grown through the engine bay. The only way to retrieve the tractor was to cut down the tree, which was sad but unavoidable.

It didn't do the tractor engine any good either.

❄ 20 ❄

Just You Wait
'Til Your Father Gets Home

Amos 2 v 4–5   Amos 9 v 11–15

Recently my electric kettle ceased to work. It was fine when I made a cup of coffee the previous evening but it was obviously deceased the following morning. Who knows what happened during the night? Fortunately I have another kettle which is not driven by electricity and during the cold weather sits on the top of my log burning stove, but as we are presently in mid-summer, it had to claim a place on the gas hob.

It had slipped my mind that this substitute kettle had an old fashioned integral whistle that warned when the water contained within the kettle was at boiling point. When preparing my first cup of tea I was reduced to searching the house for the source of the annoying whistling noise before realising that it was emanating from the kettle.

I have now purchased a new kettle which is powered by electricity and has no whistle, but has several safety features incorporated in its design.

These include an automatic cut off when the water boils and a delay of one minute after boiling before power can be reactivated. There is also a special safety design feature that makes the kettle glow with a blue light when the water is cool but glows with a red light when the water is hot – how good is that?

Our lives are inundated with warnings, my car dashboard lights up like a Christmas tree with red warning symbols until the engine starts and they are all extinguished (I hope), and my reversing sensors beep their warning progressively louder to warn me of an obstruction that draws close and I need to stop. There are warning signs all around us, the Highway Code is full of them. However there is one particular bridge in the centre of Derby which, despite an elaborate system of warnings about its low height, has claimed the roof of many high vehicles the drivers of which chose to ignore the bells, flashing lights and sirens.

So this adds another dimension to our list of, to do or not to do, choices in life, do we take notice or do we ignore the warnings?

There are times when we feel that we must test the validity of the warning's message just to ascertain if they are relevant or not. A good example is the park bench with a sign warning, 'Wet Paint'. Some people will touch the paint just to see if the paint is really wet, others will walk away and seek another bench without a sign and others will simply move the sign and sit down on the assumption that the warning only applies to other people and not to them. This is known as the, 'Only applies to others', syndrome and is commonly found in relation to road speed limits and COVID restrictions.

My mum had an array of verbal warnings that she used to significant effect. These would include, 'Do that again and you will be sorry', or 'One more word and you will be sorry', or 'If I have to tell you again you will be sorry'. The temptation was always there to push the boundaries and discover just how sorry I would be, but I have never been one for confrontational situations so I don't think that I ever dared to call her bluff, not without a robust escape plan. Some warnings were impractical to say the least, like the one that claimed that unless I behaved we would cancel our holiday to the sea side. Did mum really think that I would believe that warning? Actually I don't think I ever tested whether she would or not, the stakes were far too high.

In the Old Testament of the Bible God sent warnings of retribution to the sinful nations, through the prophets. It was their role to pass on God's words to the people warning them to repent and turn back to God or suffer the punishment. The prophet Amos lived in the middle of the 8th century BC and preached to the northern kingdom of Israel. It was a time of apparently great prosperity but this was only a veneer over underlying corruption, religious idolatry, and injustice. Amos could see that the prosperity was limited to the wealthy few and the majority suffered from poverty, injustice and oppression. God's warning was to the nation that had turned its back on God and he warned of the impending punishment that was about to descend upon them.

Amos called for justice to, 'Flow like a stream', and the wealth shared across the nation. But the warnings also contained a message of hope that God would reprieve all those who listened to his word and repented, to those he would be merciful but to those who ignored the warnings, they would be punished.

Eventually the northern kingdom of Israel was overcome by its enemies and suffered destruction, but God rebuilt the nation and rewarded those who had followed his words.

One warning of my mum's always made me smile and in later life manifested itself in my own family. When mum thought enough was enough she would warn, 'Just you wait until your dad gets home.'

The problem was that dad would just smile and wink and say, 'behave' and that was that.

✲ 21 ✲

One Man's Rubbish

Mark 5 v 1–13

I live on quite a long road (well it seems long when you walk along it), which was built in the early 1960s to accommodate some 400 new homes at that time. Since then I estimate that 90% of those homes have now been extended or structurally altered in some way, which means that a considerable number of waste skips have clanked, clattered and clanged their way up and down the road over the years. Recently several of my neighbours have employed builders to carry out work on their properties the process of which has necessitated the need for a waste skip and as the offending skip has to be positioned at the front of the property, I have had the perfect opportunity to observe the various uninvited visitors to these metal containers of potential gold.

The first in the pecking order is invariably the roving scrap metal collector (known in my day as the Rag and Bone man), who diligently sifts through the timber and wasted bags of plaster to find the smallest morsel of metal. They dance with delight when electrical wire is discovered or a length of copper pipe discarded by the plumber. Rich pickings in the world of scrap metal.

Next to arrive are those people seeking the wooden pallets on which bricks or roofing tiles had been previously delivered. These are eagerly loaded into the boot of their estate cars and squirreled away to a secret destination. I enquired from one such seeker of pallets what the future held for these discarded, sometimes intricately designed, wooden honeycombs. He informed me that he made garden furniture from them which he then sold and gave the profits to charity, which just goes to prove that one man's rubbish is someone else's gold.

Hard on the heels of the seekers of pallets come the log burning fraternity, drawn towards any length of dry unpainted timber that can be transformed into winter fuel for the log burning stove (I have one myself so I am first in line). In addition to the regular visitors to the skip there are also the, 'just in case' visitors who like to have a rummage just in case there is something useful, after all there may be a lost Van Gogh hidden under all that brick dust.

I was surprised one morning when I drew my curtains at 7.00am to see and elderly gentleman armed with a carrier bag retrieving plastic bottles, glass jam jars and other recyclable domestic items from a skip. He appeared to be rescuing anything that could have been disposed of in the regular wheelie bin and placing it in his carrier bag before jumping on his bicycle and peddling away. Perhaps he was fulfilling his own personal environmental crusade.

Back in the late 1950s waste skips were not as prevalent as they are today and as my dad was a man with a van or truck, he was often called upon to cart away someone's rubbish. He said it was a nice little earner on a wet Saturday. It made no difference if the rubbish was timber, brick, hard-core or a bed and mattress, it all went to the refuse tip on the outskirts of Bradford called Odsal Top Tip. This was an enormous depression in the landscape into which most of the city's rubbish was deposited with little or no apparent consideration for environmental management. I often went with my dad to the tip and I can recall him driving down a spiralling road through layers of foul smelling rubbish to reach the lower levels where we tipped whatever was in the back of the van or truck. There was no idea of recycling or separation of materials it was just all land fill.

In Biblical times, despite the clinical images brought to us by the Christian art, hygiene was not at the top of the agenda in the day to day life of a lower class villager. In big cities rubbish would have been jettisoned over the city wall and left to decompose but in smaller villages anything unpleasant or emitting a foul odour was dumped on the outskirts of the village creating a no go area, a foul smelling and putrid landscape.

It was into this environment of foul smelling rubbish, rotting corpses in the tombs and pigs, that we find the demoniac 'Legion' or 'Mob', the man possessed by so many demons that even his name was dictated by them. More importantly it is the place where we find Jesus. Not put off by the degradation that surrounds him, Jesus joined this tormented soul of Legion and drove out the demons that racked this man's body and destroyed his mind. Legion had been cast out by society due to his behaviour and forced to reside in the squalor and the filth where no one would reach him. In his mental turmoil he had the strength to break the chains that bound him and he would scream uncontrollably in his torment.

How many of us would turn away in disgust and fear at the sight of this apparition?

Jesus was filled with compassion and pity and drove out the demons into the pigs to give this man peace at last. Jesus was criticised for the loss of the pigs but to The Lord the saving of that tormented soul is worth much more than a herd of pigs.

Odsal Top was closed for tipping in the 1980s and much has now been reclaimed and developed. There is now a sports stadium on the site which is the home of Bradford Bulls Rugby Club (Bradford Northern in my day), and a leisure complex named after the famous

One Man's Rubbish

Yorkshire boxer Richard Dunn, who almost, but not quite, beat Casius Clay (Muhammad Ali).

It was a close match and if it wasn't for the fact the Richard got knocked out he might have won!

22

Where Were You?

Matthew 26 v 69–75

Obviously the impact of global events will depend on the generation of which we are a part, for example, the events of over one hundred years ago may have little relevance to today's youth. Many of us are aware of the Titanic disaster in 1912 but it is not likely to be a milestone event in most of our lives unless we are historians. However, the declaration of the start of World War I or II will still have a place in the memories of many people.

I suppose my memory milestones start with the coronation of our present queen but only because at the age of five years I recall the celebration rather than the event. I can distinctly recall where I was when the American President John Kennedy was assassinated in November 1963. I was fifteen years old at the time and I was in a Methodist Church Hall watching an amateur dramatics production. I went outside during the interval and everyone was talking about the assassination. I can also recall the moon landings in 1969, watching it on my, 'In law's' television because Jean and I didn't have a set. We only got married two months before and funds had not stretched to a television set.

I would consider the two most significant global events that have impacted the most on my lifeline have been the death of Princess Diana in 1997, and the Twin Towers 9/11 terrorist attack in America in 2001.

In August 1997, Jean and I were on holiday in Portugal and deliberately isolating ourselves from newspapers and television. It was not until we telephoned home to check on the family that we learned of the tragic death of Princess Diana in the accident in a French underpass. Similarly in September 2001 I was attending a meeting in Nottingham when the proceedings were interrupted by an announcement that the terrorist attack on the Twin Towers had been carried out. It would be a few days before the true impact of the event would become evident but we all knew that the effects would be life changing and long lasting, particularly in relation to security and public buildings.

There is one event that had a considerable impact on me although I could not give a specific reason why. This was the capsizing of the Ferry Spirit of Free Enterprise as it departed from Zeebrugge harbour in March 1997. Perhaps it was because Jean and I had travelled on such a vessel and could imagine what it must have been like but I knew that this would be one of my flags in my memories.

Of course personal events constantly become a memory aid when trying to establish or recall a specific happening from the past. How many times do I think, did it happen before we moved to Derby? Or did it happen before one of the girls was born? Or was it before or after I retired? I think psychiatrists refer to it as being a 'point of association', our minds lock onto an event in order to open other doors in our brain to release memories.

I am sure that the night that Jesus was arrested and his death on the cross were events that would be permanently engraved on the minds of the disciples for the rest of their lives but none more than for Peter. I wonder how many times he would relive the events that took place in that courtyard and wish that he could turn back the clock and act differently.

When Jesus told Peter that despite his best efforts Peter would deny Jesus three times before the cock crowed, Peter genuinely thought that it would never happen, but it did. Three times Peter was challenged by onlookers who accused him of being a follower of Jesus, and three times he denied that he even knew him. It was only when the cock crowed that Peter realised what he had done.

In future years when Peter would be asked, 'Where were you when Jesus was tortured and beaten?' He would remember that he was in a courtyard, hiding and denying that he even knew him. But Jesus knew that he would do just that. It was foretold and was part of the prediction of the journey that Jesus had to take. Peter had been forgiven even before his act of denial. He was part of God's plan to bring glory to his son Jesus Christ and salvation to all creation.

There was no shame for Peter or condemnation, he would meet with the risen Lord and be assured that he was the rock on which the church of Christ would be established.

So what about the milestones of the future? What will our young people of today use as their, 'Points of association'? Perhaps the pandemic of 2020, or perhaps the vivid images of man's/woman's first steps on planet Mars, or perhaps the day when robots finally take over the world?

Who knows?

✤ 23 ✤

Samuel Pepys vs Social Media

Matthew 14 v 13–21   John 6 v 25–2

Without doubt the present pandemic will form study projects for schools and universities in years to come, perhaps even in 100 or 200 years' time. You may ask how I have come to this conclusion and I can confirm that from experience our schools today study the Great Plague of 1665 and the Great Fire of London that helped to bring it to an end in 1666. When I say from experience, I don't mean that I was there at the time but I have assisted three daughters and several grandchildren to make models of London houses etc. for school projects on the subject. Even in my school days we made a cardboard model of London in the 17th century. It was so good it went on display in the school hall. We wanted to add to its authenticity by setting fire to it but the Headmaster didn't think that was a good idea.

Most of the information and knowledge of the plague and of life in general during the mid-17th century came from the writings of a man called Samuel Pepys, who was a Member of Parliament, a naval administrator and an author at that time but most importantly he kept a very concise diary. I don't think that at the time Samuel Pepys wrote his diary he would have realised how significant it would be in determining our perception of social reactions to the crisis 400 years later.

So how will historians in the future assess Pandemic 2020? Generally, in the absence of diaries (I don't know anyone who keeps a diary nowadays), I suppose social media would be the equivalent but how much of social media information could the historians of 25th century rely on as being accurate in describing what society believed at the time. After all I have come across some ludicrous miss information that would depict today's society as being, to say the least, naïve.

For example, one report stated that the entire pandemic was a secret plan by the government to get rid of 'old people'!!! As the majority of government are 'old people' it is hardly likely that such an act would successfully get through Parliament.

Another theory that was presented on a social media platform was that the vaccination that we all received contained a chemical that made our bodies 'magnetic'. Would this result in our bodies being magnetised and adhere to the nearest steel beam or column, or will bits of metal debris jump up and stick to our bodies as we walked down the street?

I am pleased to say that all these theories have

been disproved, but how many people actually believed them?

In the reading from Matthew we learn of Jesus addressing a crowd of several thousand people. He was preaching to them about the fact that the Kingdom of God was approaching and they must prepare themselves for the promise of the Messiah that would be fulfilled. They have the opportunity to be one with God to have their sins forgiven an opportunity for a new life on earth and everlasting life in the kingdom of heaven. They were being offered freedom, something that had been out of their grasp for centuries.

Jesus sealed his message by performing a great miracle by feeding all those present from a tiny food source, not only to provide sufficient food for the assembled crowd but also baskets of food left over.

The crowd were elated and eager to chase after Jesus for more, but in John's gospel, John 6 verses 25–29, we learn that it wasn't more of the good news message they were after, it was another meal that they demanded from Jesus. They believed in the physical sustenance but not all believed in the spiritual revival. The people asked where they could get this bread which Jesus spoke about and Jesus replied, 'What God wants you to do is to believe in the one he has sent'. (Verse 29). Later in verse 35 Jesus told them 'I am the bread of life'.

This was a problem that would haunt the Jewish nation throughout history. Paul in his letters to the

Corinthians set out his theology of justification by faith, being one with God by believing in Jesus Christ. Through believing in him we become like him and live a way of life that will be righteous in God's eyes. The Jews believed that the only way to righteousness with God was through compliance with the Law of Moses. The problem with that theology was that it was impossible to comply with the Law so it only accentuated the sins of the people. Through the death and resurrection of Jesus Christ God made the ultimate sacrifice that paid the price of all our sins overriding the Jewish Law. It is through faith and belief in Jesus Christ not through any act of our own that we receive salvation and everlasting life in the kingdom of heaven.

There are others who will try to persuade us otherwise, putting forward alternative theories even the conspiracy theories. Some will offer scientific explanations, archaeological solutions and alternative celestial powers but they are all false and irrelevant. The only true message is that Jesus Christ is the Son of God, he died on the cross and was raised from the dead and now he rules at the right hand of God the Father.

We started with a theory of being magnetised by the COVID vaccination. In a television programme called The Planets by Prof Brian Cox, he explained that billions of years ago when the earth was formless, a gas giant planet called Jupiter formed and travelled across the universe destroying all in its path and on a collision course with earth. However, its mission was halted when the sun ignited into a fire ball and the magnetic gravity field from another gas giant called Saturn pulled Jupiter into another orbit. This left the earth to use its own magnetic gravity field to develop its own orbit and atmosphere and get on with life.

Well done Saturn – we owe you one, but it is all in Genesis.

24

A Night at the Pictures

1 Samuel 17 v 1–6 and 48–50

It is some time now since I went to the cinema, after all due to COVID the opportunity to visit such places has not existed. I think the last film that I viewed was 'Bohemian Rhapsody', the story of the rock band, 'Queen' and their lead singer Freddy Mercury. Prior to this I watched, 'A Star is Born' and 'Dunkirk'.

I must say that a visit to the cinema today is quite an experience and something totally different to that of the past. In modern cinemas the seats are ergonomically designed to enable you to recline in comfort and watch the screen with the correct angle for the line of vision. There is also the provision of a cup holder and a table which can be folded away if not required. Obviously there is a comprehensive array of drinks and confectionary to purchase which can be accommodated in the cup holder or on the table. The screen is so wide and the clarity of the images displayed is so precise, that you actually feel as though you are in the film with the actors. However, it is possibly the sound system that has the greatest impact. It is loud, but not distorted and in films such as 'Dunkirk' you can be excused if you reactively dodge the bullets and bombs as they zip past your ears. It is certainly a long way from the 'picture palaces' of my youth in the 1960s.

In the suburb of Bradford where I lived, there were three small picture houses, the Essoldo, the Elite and the Arcadian, all within a good walk of my home. These cinemas tended to present the lesser known or older films whereas if you preferred to watch a bigger or a latest film, it required a trolley bus ride into Bradford centre to the Gaumont or the Odeon. Even bigger films would require a journey to Leeds where my mum, dad, and I watched 'The Sound of Music' with Julie Andrews (she was in the film, she didn't go with us).

My favourites were the two local cinemas. They had double seats at the rear of the auditorium for courting couples and you viewed the screen through a fog of cigarette smoke that was pierced by the bright shaft of light from the projection box. Often the film would jam in the projector which resulted in the images on the screen distorting and then melting as the heat from the bulb in the projector destroyed the film strip. The audience had to wait (impatiently), for the film to be repaired before it could continue.

Despite the breakdowns, the smoke and the disgusting smell of cheap air freshener, a visit to the pictures was good value. I recall paying 1/6d (15p) and for that I got two films, an A film and a B film. The A film was the main attraction and the B film was a lesser known film often an Alfred Hitchcock mystery. In addition the films were repeated throughout the evening so if you happen to arrive late and missed the start of the film you could just stay in your seat until the film came round again and see the bit that you missed.

I particularly enjoyed the film 'Ben Hur' which, when first released was spectacular to say the least. It was one of those, 'Cast of thousands' films that became popular, and was full of breath-taking scenes of action and battles of Biblical proportions, including a thirty minute spectacular chariot race around a Roman arena. It starred Charlton Heston and was directed by William Wyler who was a master of creating an atmosphere of tension and expectation before the big scene explodes into action.

In the Bible, the writer of 1 Samuel 17, gives a vivid description of the impending battle between the armies of the Israelites and the Philistines. We are left in no doubt as to the power of the Philistines and we can almost feel the fear in the hearts of King Saul's Israelite soldiers. The words create a mental picture of that Valley of Elah with the opposing armies facing each other from opposite hillsides, shouting their battle cries, beating their swords against their shields and demonstrating their power and strength in an attempt to terrorise their opponents. The pressure was building and it was almost at the point of exploding into a full battle.

King Saul was facing a dilemma, he knew that God was on his side but the power of the Philistines left him wandering how his Israelite army could possibly defeat such an adversary. Then an opportunity unexpectedly presented itself. Goliath, the biggest, strongest most powerful and fearsome soldier in all the armies threw down a challenge of one to one combat, winner takes all, loser loses all but who could overcome this powerhouse of a man? David seemed an unlikely candidate but we forget that he was filled with the power and strength of God and God needs no sword or shield or armour, all that was needed was David's faith, a stone and a sling to destroy the Philistine giant.

God's power overshadows anything that we consider powerful and his power will overcome all that stands in the way of his love. The most fearsome weapons mean nothing, hatred will be overcome and God's power will prevail.

I can remember one occasion when I took the girl who lived next door to the Arcadian picture house to see the film 'Easter Parade'. She was mad on musicals and I thought I could impress her, but, I only had enough money for the ticket so it meant that we had to walk home. It wasn't raining when we set off, but it was when came home.

Strangely we never went out together again after that.

25

100 + 7

Luke 7 v 1–10   Matthew 18 v 21–22

I noticed recently a sporting event called 100 Cricket. As I have not previously heard of this, I was intrigued to know the difference between traditional Cricket and 100 Cricket, so I tuned in to the finals of the tournament on television. It transpired to be an adaptation of the traditional test match cricket but each team only has 100 balls to bowl out the opposing team, who must score as many runs as possible in the same number of balls (I hope you followed all that). The result was an exciting game with lots of runs being scored and lots of wickets falling, but it made me contemplate, as with the game, how our lives are influenced by the number 100.

When a batsperson scores one hundred runs, the spectators stand and applaud their achievement and in turn the batsman or woman acknowledges the praise by waving their bat in the air in great adulation. It is all about reaching that special target of a century. Similarly a century also depicts a passage of time. We live in the 21st century which places us in a one hundred year time slot in the greater calendar of life. If someone is fortunate enough to live throughout that time slot to the ripe old age of one hundred, they can look forward to receiving a congratulatory telegram from the Queen or King. I suppose it would probably be a text message or email nowadays.

The influence of that magical number has an even more far reaching impact on our everyday life. Our monetary system revolves around one hundred pence in the pound, or one hundred cents in a dollar etc. Likewise with the metric system of measurement, millimetres, centimetres, metres and so on, along with weights and volumes. There is no doubt that what-ever we do we just can't get away from that number. I can recall in the 1960s when the M1 motorway first opened, it was an inauguration into high social circles to drive at 100 miles per hour (there was no speed restriction in those days), in your car or even more significantly, on your motorbike. It even had its own slogan, 'Do a ton on the M1'.

In sport it is not only cricket that relies on the one hundred rules, athletics is also one of its victims. Are you aware that Usain Bolt can run 100m in 9.58 seconds? If he maintained that speed for one hour he would cover almost 36km. I wonder if that would enhance or lessen his chances of receiving a telegram from the Queen or King.

Even in the arena of the battle field we cannot escape the gravitational attraction of one hundred,

England and France were embroiled in a 100 year war during the middle ages, a conflict between the English Plantagenet monarch and the French royal House of Valois. In the Roman army there was an officer rank of Centurion who was responsible for one hundred soldiers under his command. In those days the rank of Centurion had to be earned and he would be battle experienced and probably battle scarred.

It is for these reasons that the Centurion's approach to Jesus in Luke 7 verses 1–10 is significant, the Roman soldiers were no friends of the Jews and vice versa, however this Centurion chose to approach Jesus and ask for help. In addition his appeal was on behalf of his servant, not usually a concern of a Centurion, servants were generally expendable, but this man showed pity and most of all faith and belief in the Son of God and it was through his faith that the servant was healed. The Centurion did not acknowledge or try to use the authority bestowed on him by the Roman occupation but humbled himself before Christ to beg for Jesus's intervention and healing power. He knew that only God could carry out such miracles.

Strangely in the Bible the number 100 loses out to another number, that of 7. Number 7 has far more authority in Biblical terms than any other, being used 735 times throughout the scriptures. God created the universe in seven days and declared that the seventh day (the Sabbath) was to be a day of rest, so the number seven signifies completion and perfection. It also represents longevity and is a symbol of everlasting.

In Matthew's gospel Peter asks Jesus how many times he must forgive his brother who has sinned against him. Jesus replies that seven times is not enough and seventy times seven represents eternity. Forgiveness has no limit or boundary and must continue for all time.

In the book of Revelation the vision reveals seven churches, seven angels, seven seals, seven trumpets, plagues and thunders. Let us not forget that seven trumpets played by seven Priests for seven days brought down the walls of Jericho (Joshua 6) and seven loaves of bread fed many thousands of people, leaving baskets of food left over (Matthew 15).

My particular favourite is that seven represents the four corners of the world brought together by the Father, Son and Holy Spirit.

Many years ago when I was a bricklayer, we had a magical target of laying one thousand bricks in a day, a target which I confess was rarely if ever achieved. The significance was that if laying one thousand bricks was achieved we earned a bonus of two shillings (10p) on the day's pay.

Bear in mind that an apprentice bricklayer's pay was £3.10s.0d. (£3.50) per week so there was an incentive.

26

The Kitchen Cabinet

1 Kings 17 v 8–24

I enjoy watching programmes on television where craftsmen and women restore antiques. I know the programmes are for television and what we see is engineered for entertainment but I still find them interesting. Recently a cabinet maker/ joiner restored a 20th century kitchen cabinet and as I watched I realised that we had a very similar cabinet in our back room when I was a lad.

My dad built a low level long cupboard unit across the length of the external wall in our terrace house. It fit just under the window sill so mum could do her baking and enjoy the view at the same time. I say enjoy the view with tongue in cheek as the view was our back yard and the backs of the row of houses opposite. I used to sit on the cupboard by the window and count the number of bags that the coal man delivered and then tell mum. At one end of dad's cupboard was the kitchen sink which was housed in its own cupboard with folding doors that we could close off when it was not in use. The sink was an earthenware Belfast style with an integral draining board. When I was young I would sit on the draining board with my feet in the sink and mum would wash me. If anyone came into the room I would pull the doors shut and hide so that no one would see me without any clothes on.

I can remember dad bringing home our first refrigerator. He had removed it from a house that he was altering and no one wanted it so dad brought it home and installed it in the long cupboard. The fridge was only small and worked on gas rather than electricity. It had a small door at the front and a grill at the top and at the bottom. As a lad I could never understand why a fridge which was cold emitted warm air from the top grill. Dad often brought things home that were surplus or not wanted from houses where he was working. He once brought home a cooking range, similar to an 'Aga' cooker and ripped out the old Yorkshire range in the back room and installed the new one. It was really too big for our house but it did provide hot water, heated the house and provided the cooking oven and hot plates on top. When dad filled it up with smokeless fuel it got so hot that the little fridge under the long cupboard couldn't keep up with keeping things cool.

One thing that dad did not bring home was the kitchen unit that was similar to the restored cabinet on television. Mum and dad bought this from a shop in Bradford centre and it was delivered in a van. It was placed between the end of dad's long cupboard and the back door. Mum loved it and it was her favourite piece of furniture after her glass fronted display cabinet. The kitchen unit was about 6ft (1.8m) tall (which meant that mum could not reach the top), and was cream with bright green doors. It had a cupboard at the top and bottom, with a drop down door in the middle which revealed access to shelves and pigeon holes inside. The most magical part was a retractable section that pulled out to form a worktop to enable food to be prepared using ingredients stored in the drop down section. After use the worktop would effortlessly slide back into the unit and out of sight. It even had small stool so mum could sit down while she made a cake. It was like something out of The Ideal Home Exhibition. It was everything that a 1950s back room kitchen needed.

I wonder what a Biblical kitchen would have looked like. In 1 Kings 17 we learn of a poor widow who was searching for wood to light a fire to cook a meal. The fire would probably be surrounded by a circle of stones that would heat up to act as an oven. The water she needed came from a well and there was no necessity for cupboards to store the ingredients as all she needed was a bowl and a jar. She was in the grip of a famine caused by a drought and her situation was so dire that she had resigned herself to the fact that she and her son where going to die from starvation. Imagine her dilemma when Elijah first asks for water then asks for a meal that would take all she had. Should she serve Elijah and by doing so certainly seal the fate of both her and her son, or should she deny Elijah and possibly prolong the lives of her and her son for a little longer. She knew that Elijah was a man of God and she also knew that it was God's will that she should serve him, so she did as he asked and sacrificed what she had for him. Her faith and obedience were rewarded and she and her son were saved not only from starvation but also from her son's illness.

God rewards those who hear and obey.

Mum's favourite piece of furniture was her glass fronted display cabinet. Her feelings for it surpassed all other material aspects in the house and it was her pride and joy. She collected miniature wine bottles, tiny replicas of the real thing and they were all arranged on display in the glass fronted display cabinet, which was located in the front room, a domain from which all were prohibited apart from on special occasions.

However, one day a set of wrought iron gates for one of dad's jobs were delivered and due to their size they had to come through the front door until such time as dad could remove them. The gates rested against the back of the settee directly opposite the glass fronted display cabinet.

The Kitchen Cabinet

A young boy, excited at the opportunity to enter into the forbidden sanctuary of the front room, launched himself onto the settee which in turn moved backwards in response to the impact. The iron gates slowly moved from their state of rest and energy was converted into movement.

When iron meets a glass fronted display cabinet it results in an awfully loud crash.

❄ 27 ❄

The Kitchen Table

Matthew 26 v 17–30

After writing about our kitchen cabinet I had a conversation with a good friend who shared some of his thoughts generated by my recollections, on his family life when he was a young lad. As so often happens, the conversation opened doors in my mind giving access to further memories of my childhood. In addition to the before mentioned kitchen cabinet, the kitchen table took a central role in everyday life in our household.

It was a square wooden table which at one time would have been highly polished but by the time my memories had caught up with it most of the polish and the dark stain had worn off giving it a patchwork appearance with bare wood showing through. Generally it remained as a square but at such times as Christmas there were two extendable sections at either end that made it into a rectangle giving more space for bigger dishes and bowls. Obviously its predominant role was for meal times but the kitchen table had many more uses. It was a general depository for a multitude of objects that should have been placed in cupboards or drawers but just dropping them on the table was far more convenient. These objects included tins of hairspray and dad's Brylcreem (the mirror was on the wall next to the table), school books not needed until the following week, dad's bills and receipts, mum's expired shopping lists and my toys cast out through boredom. Eventually mum would have a mini tantrum and we all had to clear our things off the table.

For a young lad with an active imagination the table could often metamorphosis into a range of exciting experiences. When overturned and an old blanket spread across the upturned legs the table would become a tent that would accommodate a picnic with imaginary friends. It became a pirate ship with some of dad's cardboard tubes as cannons protruding from the sides. It became a cowboy chuck wagon constantly being attacked by wild tribes of Indians, and if two chairs were added at one end, one for the driver and the other for the imaginary friend, the table changed into to a heavy haulage lorry delivering coal to the entire neighbourhood.

Chairs could also change their appearance. By laying two chairs down with the chair backs together, I could crawl inside and it became a racing car tearing round Silverstone race track at 100 miles an hour with authentic sound effects being generated from the back of my throat. Alternatively it became a space ship and

I was Dan Dare chasing Ming across the universe (you needed to listen to the radio to understand), or my favourite being a submarine under the sea like Jules Verne's Captain Nemo.

Undoubtedly the table and chairs was an amazing outlet for imaginary adventures but in real time upturned tables and chairs did not go well and were quite disruptive to everyday household activities. At those times other alternatives had to be sought, usually cardboard boxes. It is well known that you can give an expensive present to a young child and initially the cardboard container receives more attention than the contents. There is something about a large cardboard box that compels a child to climb inside. They can be climbing Everest or exploring underground caves and tunnels all in the safety of a cardboard box on the kitchen floor.

In Matthew's account of the last supper the table never gets a mention but it is central as a witness to the drama that unfolds. The artist Leonardo de Vinci in his portrayal of The Last Supper depicts the table as being a long trestle covered with plates, dishes and cups with the disciples sat around. It was the Passover meal when God's act of delivering the Jewish nation out of slavery is remembered. Initially the disciples would be happy, excited, gathering together to share in the traditional Passover meal. They would be laughing and joking, chatting while they waited for the ceremonial start of the meal.

For Jesus it was a table of contemplation, as he looked across the table at each of the disciples he would have contemplated how their lives would change in just a few hours' time. Peter would deny him, Thomas would doubt him and Judas would betray him.

The time came for the mood to change, the frivolity discarded as inappropriate, the darkness of disbelief and despair collaborating with fear engulfed them. Which one would betray Jesus, an act that would unavoidably take Jesus to his death on the cross?

When the meal concluded they all left into the garden and the table was left alone dishevelled with the plates, bowls and cups scattered. They would never return, the table would never witness the disciples gathering in the same way again. They would next meet with the resurrected Lord.

It was a lonely place around the discarded table. It had witnessed the final act of communion before Jesus's death but an act that will live on in the presence of all believers for all time.

As I grew a little older the attraction of imaginary lorries, ships and other roles offered by the upturned table diminished. However, other opportunities presented themselves. By extending the table at each end and fitting a net across the centre, it was transformed into an Olympic table tennis arena used by all the family. Not only was that introduced but dad also acquired a quarter sized snooker table which fitted on top of the kitchen table to enable many world championship tournaments to be held in our kitchen.

28

Birthday Cards and Christmas Presents

Matthew 2

On my calendar that hangs on my kitchen wall, every month of the year displays at least one birthday and on many months displays multiple birthday celebrations. The most prolific months are September and October which combined produce no less than eight of these notable dates.

It's not that I begrudge people having birthdays, after all I have one myself, it's the fact that I have to remember them, not just the date but also in most cases the relevant age of the recipient. Getting the age correct is essential so as not to offend the birthday person, for example, if I send a twelve years card and it should be a thirteen year one the result can be devastating. You are not grown up at twelve but you are at thirteen. Similarly if I accidentally send an eightieth card and it should be seventy nine resounding repercussions can be experienced.

In addition to remembering dates I also have great difficulty in choosing the card that I consider to be suitable. I avoid what my dad would describe as, 'Sloppy verses', I am wishing someone a happy birthday not declaring my undying love. Similarly I usually divert my attention away from the, 'humorous' cards, although it has been known for me to be sympathetic towards the satirical humour. Pastimes and interest subjects are usually a safe bet, football for the boys, horses and horse riding for the girls, wine bottles and bubbles for the more grown up ladies and Land Rovers for the enthusiasts (grown up but not grown up). Finding the card nowadays is a challenge particularly during COVID when many of the specialist card shops have remained closed. Often the internet has again come to the rescue and provided a solution. Several dedicated sites will produce a bespoke design that can be printed at the touch of a button or alternatively posted directly to the birthday address. I received a birthday card the front of which displayed a picture of my classic car with me posing alongside. It now adorns the fridge door with two magnets.

Christmas cards are a much easier proposition. Traditional nativity scenes and snow covered countryside vistas with the occasional Robins can be sent with confidence. Even a picture of a classic car set against a backdrop of a quintessential rural village post office all covered in copious layers of snow is also acceptable.

Both Christmas and birthdays have another stressful common denominator that is, presents. The older people get the more difficult it seems to be to choose the most suitable gift. When children are in their younger years it is relatively easy to follow the trends of the craze that predominates at that time. I can recall purchasing various items in the 'My Little Pony' range along with 'Barbie Dolls', 'Care Bears' and 'Bob the Builder' all with the confidence that excitement would run high when the wrappings were removed. However that level of excitement is more difficult to achieve when the recipient is much older.

I have discovered that serious consultation is necessary before any item of clothing is purchased as a gift. The style of football shirts change more frequently than teenage socks and it is almost guaranteed that the item bought will be the wrong one. Equally any item relating to computers or information technology requires a much higher level of understanding than I can provide so specialised advice, almost certainly from a teenager, will be required.

It seems strange to talk about Christmas when at the time of writing this reflection there are just over twelve weeks to the great day but a recent incident made me consider just when did the visitors from the east in Matthew's gospel actually set off on their journey to the stable. Modern interpretation of the scriptures suggest that they arrived after Jesus had been taken by Joseph and Mary to Egypt to avoid the wrath of Herod, but how long did it take them to travel?

They had no motorised transport, no accurate maps, and no fixed destination. Their only guidance was by the stars and one particular constellation that they felt compelled to follow. Recognisable roads were not available and progress would be painfully slow. The Bible gives no indication as to where they came from apart from it was in the east but geographically it is probable that crossing mountain ranges and negotiating narrow mountain passes would have been unavoidable. It could have taken them years to reach their destination so, they would certainly have set off by now.

They carried with them gifts but possibly not the kind of gifts we would have thought appropriate to take a young child. They carried gifts of Gold, Frankincense and Myrrh.

Gold was the most precious metal fit for a King and recognised as the gift for all royalty. Frankincense at that time was more valuable than gold and was obtained from sacred trees only found in the Arabian Peninsula. It was highly sought after and represented Royalty and holiness, its sweet smelling perfume was used in palaces and temples. Myrrh was also produced from the resin from a specific tree found in Arabia and Northeast Africa. It was possibly more valuable than both gold and frankincense but unlike frankincense it had a bitter and sharp perfume. It was used to prepare a body for the tomb after death.

I was in the Coop supermarket the other day, in the queue for the till and I started a conversation with the person behind me (as you do). Her basket was full of packets of Sage and Onion stuffing and jars of Cranberries. Flippantly I mused that it must be a big Turkey to take all that stuffing and she explained that it was going to her friend in Saudi Arabia ready for their Christmas celebration (apparently sage and onion stuffing is not readily available).

She was obviously well organised and already getting prepared for Christmas I almost asked her if she had written all her Christmas cards yet but restrained my curiosity. I did ask her if her friend in Saudi had put the sprouts on to boil yet – she said she didn't know but she would ask her next time they talked.

29

The Fishes That Didn't Get Away

Luke 5 v 1–11

I have never really been an angling enthusiast, too little happens in too long a time, as far as I am concerned. However, when I was around 9 or 10 years old, an elderly neighbour used to take me fishing in an attempt to instil some interest in me for the sport. His name was Mr Stansfield (I never did know his first name), and he lived further along the terrace. He provided a rod, reel, keep net and a wooden box with flip up lid. The box could also be used as a seat. Inside the box I would keep my sandwiches and drink, and a metal tin with a gauze lid in which I stored the maggots used for bait.

I accompanied Mr Stansfield on several fishing trips but I cannot remember ever catching a fish, I don't know what I would have done if I had caught one. At the end of each trip we would empty any surplus maggots from the tin, into the river and give the fish a treat. On one occasion I failed to follow this procedure and a couple of weeks later, when preparing for another fishing adventure, I opened the tin only to find that the maggots had all changed into hundreds of flies, all trying to escape from the tin at once. This phenomenon did nothing to encourage my interest in the sport of angling. Sadly Mr Stansfield died and I technically inherited the rod, reel, keep net and wooden box with the flip up lid containing the metal tin with a gauze top. I say inherited, actually no one else wanted them.

Several years later I befriended a lad called Ian who lived in an area of Bradford called Chellow Dene, a salubrious part of the city that encircled the Chellow Dene Reservoir. Ian suggested that I brought my fishing rod over to his house and we could spend the day fishing in the reservoir, so it came to pass that I, along with all my angling equipment, boarded a number 80 bus and joined him at the water's edge. This time I avoided the possibility of recreating the tin of flies by excavating an area of Ian's dad's garden and collecting worms that I was sure the fish would be attracted to.

Predictively we never caught a single fish, in fact the reverse was the case as we were the ones that got caught. We had never heard of a fishing licence until the Warden approached us and asked to see it. It transpired that no one could fish in the reservoir unless they obtained a fishing licence and a permit and we had neither. It required intervention by Ian's father, who seemed very influential in these matters, to sort it all out.

It is interesting to note that there are very few references to fishing in the Old Testament but in the New Testament there are plenty of references. Perhaps that's a result of the geography of the Old Testament compared to that of the New Testament. The Old Testament action generally takes place in the wilderness, the desert, or the lush plains of the Promised Land where farming, vineyards and arable production is predominant. It seems a long way from the fishing opportunities of the New Testament around Lake Galilee. Perhaps that's why bread is good in the Old Testament but if you want fish and chips you need the New Testament.

In Luke's gospel Jesus told the disciples that they would become fishers of men, which sounds like a strange terminology to use when talking about saving people's souls.

So like the parables that Jesus would use later in his ministry, using terminology that the disciples could understand caught their attention and they accepted that this carpenter's son knew them and their skills. They were unlikely to respond in the same way to a deeply theological question but Jesus was not satisfied with using the right language he wanted to demonstrate his power. Take your boats out to the deep water, he told them, and cast your nets.

Now there are two types of fishing, trawler fishing as with the boats from Grimsby (a net drawn through deep water catching fish on the bottom). Or casting a net in shallow water to catch fish closer to the surface and this second one was Peter and his friend's speciality. So when Jesus sent them to the deep water it should have been a fruitless exercise. The fish would be too low down for their nets to reach them. However the nets came up full to bursting.

Jesus showed that not only did he know the fishermen, he also had the power to change all the rules. The fishermen left their nets and their way of life and followed Jesus and his promise that they would be fishers of men was fulfilled. But where would they find this rich harvest? We find a clue when we read prophesies that went before. The Messiah came to set the prisoner free, let the blind see and the deaf hear and let those in chains be free from their burdens. Where do we find such souls? In the deepest darkest depths of suffering and despair. It will take a strong and determined arm to raise these souls from the darkest depths into the light of Jesus Christ but Jesus knew the disciples.

My close encounter with the fishing licence dampened any enthusiasm towards angling and it was only a short time after, that I placed an advertisement in the Bradford Telegraph and Argos newspaper saying, 'For Sale fishing rod, reel, keep net and wooden box with a flip up lid containing a metal tin with a gauze top.'
I received £5 for the lot.

✤ 30 ✤

The Apprentice

Matthew 17 v 14–21

Several of my grandchildren have passed or are passing through the new apprenticeship educational process and two who have now completed their training have secured full time jobs. Apprenticeships are a very successful way of learning a profession through hands on activities in the workplace under the supervision of fully qualified and experienced mentors. They are an excellent way of developing a profession, learning skills and acquiring a trade by actually being involved with doing the job. But apprenticeships are not new, in fact they have been around for centuries.

In the Middle Ages the parents or guardian of their child would have negotiated with an employer to accept him as an apprentice (in those days it was predominantly boys). The apprentice would leave home to live with the guild master who would be responsible for his training. Apprentices would receive board and lodging but no salary or wages. Neither was their life easy, it would involve hard work and often harsh treatment. Boys as young as 12 years old would be sent away from home for up to 7 years without any chance of returning until they were freed from their apprenticeship, many never saw home or family again. Only a fortunate few ever became guild masters in their own right.

It has to be said that board and lodgings were not what we would recognise as such today. Invariably it would consist of a bed on the shop floor or a space under the stair leading up to the first floor factory. An apprentice was expected to be, 'At work' all the time including sleeping. Meals would have been frugal and due to malnourishment and accidents at work, the mortality rate among young apprentices was high. It was common for the apprentice and their family, to enter into an agreement called an indenture, in which there was a commitment that the apprentice would remain with the guild master for the agreed length of time and severe punishment would result if the agreement was broken. In those days there was a thin line between apprenticeship and slavery.

The first recorded national apprenticeship scheme was introduced in 1563 and was unchanged until, due to concerns over the exploitation of young apprentices, it was finally amended some 250 years later. It was not until the start of the 20th century when the apprenticeship schemes were redefined and became more popular. Even I can claim to have served an apprenticeship (not in the Middle Ages), in the mid-1960s as a bricklayer. I served five years starting when I was 16 years old, became an 'Improver' at 18 years and a 'Craftsman' at 21 years old.

Even though I worked for my father I was not exempt from the menial tasks such as making the tea, fetching from the local shop, or being sent to find a left handed screw driver or a right handed hammer. I never did find a 375 degree drain pipe bend or a self-emptying bucket but the suppliers had a good laugh at my expense. Although I never experienced it I have heard of several joiners apprentices complain of tea mugs being glued to the workbench prior to being lifted to the lips.

The benefit of the modern apprenticeships is that they are interfaced with an educational provider such as a university or college which means that the practical skills learnt in the workplace are reinforced by the academic skills and in most cases modern techniques, developed in the lecture theatre.

In many ways, in the Bible the disciples could be recognised as being Biblical apprentices. Jesus called them from their previous lives as fishermen, physicians, tax collectors and such and led them to be disciples of The Lord. For almost three years they had lived and learned from Jesus. They had struggled with the mysteries of God, the complexities of Jesus's mission, the hypocrisy of the Pharisees, but most of all the love and caring that emanated from Jesus.

In Matthew's gospel we learn that after witnessing the events on the top of the mountain, observing the meeting between Moses, Elijah and Jesus and hearing the voice of God, the disciples must have felt that they had reached their goal, they now knew it all because they had seen it all. As they descended from their mountain top experience reality descended upon them. They tried and failed to drive out the demon from the man's son and yet with one word Jesus healed the boy.

They pleaded with Jesus to tell them what they had done wrong and why they had failed when they tried to heal to boy. Jesus's reply was short – unbelief. They did not yet have the belief and the faith to drive out the demon and heal the boy. Soon they would, with the help of the Holy Spirit, God will give them the faith that they will require but until then they must learn, trust and obey.

When I was reaching the end of my apprenticeship as a bricklayer, one of our 'wise' old labourers took me to one side and gave me some advice. He told me that when I was 21 years old and officially a craftsman, I should leave and go to another company. He then explained that in the eyes of other staff, once an apprentice always an apprentice and it is difficult to be accepted as anything else. I laughed, ignored him and went and got married.

My wife told me that I should look for another job as there were greater opportunities elsewhere. Four months later I started work in a new job in Local Authority. My wife was obviously far more persuasive than the 'wise' old labourer.